THE WINTER STORM

A JACKLYN STONE THRILLER

SUSAN SPECHT ORAM

Published by SOS Communications LLC in 2025

www.susanspechtoram.com

First Edition

ISBN: 979-8-9926053-0-3 (paperback)

ISBN: 979-8-9891982-9-0 (e-book)

❀ Created with Vellum

PREVIOUSLY

PREVIOUSLY IN:

SHORE LODGE

Jacklyn Stone, a grieving widow and garden store owner, is admitted by her greedy son to Shore Lodge, a secure psychiatric facility. She must escape to rescue her dog and reclaim her home.

BY MIDNIGHT

Jacklyn Stone helps friends gather money to keep a debt collector at bay, but the clock is ticking, and it's a race against time.

AT SHORE LODGE
NURSE WRIGHT

Nurse Wright rubbed her temples and stood in the doorway of Shore Lodge's second-floor dayroom. Speakers in the hallway spewed out holiday tunes, and a fake Christmas tree sprayed with an evergreen scent was giving her a headache.

She crossed her arms and frowned because tomorrow was Christmas Eve, but a surprise inspection last week had generated mountains of paperwork. Her troubles were due to Jacklyn Stone, a previous resident who escaped, bringing close scrutiny from authorities.

Her thoughts turned to her two upcoming days off. She'd serve a special dinner tomorrow night to family and friends, and the smell of hot cider and cinnamon would permeate the house. Christmas Eve would be a night to remember. She tapped a toe, eager to exit the stark florescent-lit facility and go grocery shopping, which meant taking a ferry from Cedar Island to Millersville.

The elevator doors opened, and a short activity aide appeared wearing a red apron over a green top and pants. She led a middle-aged woman and three teenage girls in red sweaters decorated with reindeer into the dayroom. Bells around their ankles jingled with each step.

Nurse Wright turned off the television and smiled at two gray haired women sitting on a couch holding hands. Nodding to residents sitting slack-jawed, dozing in vinyl easy chairs, she wanted to climb in her car and join the ferry line before it grew too long. Otherwise, she'd have to wait for the next boat. She glanced at a wall clock, noting she had a half hour until the next ferry left, which was cutting it close.

She clapped her hands and said in a loud voice, "We have a special treat today. Our visitors will sing holiday songs for us."

Bells jingled as the singing group walked to the front of the room. They lined up and began to sing. Nurse Wright nodded to the activity aide and returned to her desk, where she slayed the mighty dragons of paperwork, and picked up her purse.

As she strode to the elevator, an aide in her thirties stopped her and said, "Could I take Christmas Eve off to be with my family? It'd mean a lot to them."

Nurse Wright tapped her lower lip. "That'd leave us

short staffed." She glanced toward the dayroom. Her residents on the second floor were docile, now that Jacklyn Stone wasn't around to rile them up. She shrugged. "Go ahead. We'll be fine. Nothing ever happens on Christmas Eve, and it'll be quiet. Enjoy your time with your family."

1

JACKLYN STONE

I lean across a table at Gigi's Café and pat my friend Mary's arm, where streaks of yellow and blue paint are smeared on her denim work shirt. She was painting a canvas when I called and said we had to go out for breakfast right away. I say, "Something's been bothering me, and I've got an idea. Will you help me?"

A smile spreads across her face. "Your last idea was to rescue Buddy. What have you cooked up now?"

I say in a low voice, "I want to help the people I left behind at Shore Lodge."

She cocks her head. "How? I can't imagine you stepping foot in that place again."

"Here's what I'm thinking. Four people in the psych ward were admitted against their will by family, but I'm sure they're of sound mind. I want to help them be released, so they can start over. What do you think?"

She shakes her head. "You can't interfere with families' wishes."

I grip the table edge. "They can revoke their durable power of attorney, like I did, and get their lives back. I hear Shore Lodge will be short staffed on Christmas Eve, making it an ideal time to slip in and see my friends."

Mary sits back. "I'm not sure. Christmas Eve is tomorrow, and we need more time to prepare. It's probably not a good idea to fly off on a whim."

The aroma of fresh ground coffee and warm scones wafts past. Christmas tunes are playing, and I tap a toe to "Jingle Bells." Karina, the owner of the café, sets down plates with scones and slices of quiche, and we dive in. I nibble at a warm scone and slather butter and jam on my next bite. The taste is so good, it makes me moan.

I clear my throat. "I've been thinking long and hard about the best approach. These people are mentally with it, but their families didn't consult with them before sticking them in the secure unit. They deserve to have a voice in where they live."

Mary sets down her fork. "We can't meddle in other people's lives, and we're not doctors. Maybe they need to be there, but only their doctors know why they were admitted. Fred would have a fit if he heard you talking like this."

I bite my lip. Mary's husband Fred is an attorney, and he helped me change my durable power of attorney after I escaped from Shore Lodge. Wiping my mouth on a napkin, I say, "They deserve a choice and a chance to leave."

Mary sips coffee and eyes me over the rim of her cup before setting it down. "I suggest we leave well enough alone. You're busy enough with your building project. You don't have time for shenanigans like this."

I swallow my last bite of quiche and say, "No one should be cooped up against their will if they're capable of living on their own. I've got to return to Shore Lodge and give these people a chance to leave, if they want."

She drains her cup and sets it down. "Have you talked with these residents you want to rescue, since you came home?"

I snort. "Nurse Wright won't allow phone calls on the staff line, and their families took away their phones when they were admitted, so there's no way for me to call. I sent a card to Florence, but it came back with big black letters saying, 'Return to Sender.'

Karina, the café owner, comes by with a pot of coffee. Her short pink hair accentuates her chiseled cheekbones. She says, "Refills?"

Mary says, "Yes, please. It seems it's my job to prevent Jacklyn from going to jail."

The diamond in Karina's nose sparkles as she pours steaming hot coffee. She says, "What's going on? Anything I can do to help?"

Mary and I exchange a quick glance. I say, "When you

get a chance, come over and join us. We're about to tackle a difficult task, and we could use your input."

Karina says, "I'll be back. It sounds exciting and mysterious." She glides away to serve other tables.

I say to Mary, "If I were still trapped in Shore Lodge's secure second floor, I'd want someone to come in and help me."

"We'll need Fred to weigh in on this."

Karina slides into a seat and smiles at us. "What's going on?"

I swallow and say, "I have a plan to free a few residents from Shore Lodge who I don't think should be there. If the four of them want to go, that is. We'll go on Christmas Eve."

Karina's mouth falls open, and she runs a hand through her hair. "Tomorrow is Christmas Eve, which doesn't leave us much time. Why don't you wait a week?"

The din in the café quiets, and I look around the room, waving to people I know. Flash is breakfasting alone by a window. He grins and waves back. A woman wearing pink workout gear nods to me and leans across the table, handing her friend with dark curly hair a paperback book. My neighbor Bernard Frackus stands at the front counter. He looks over his dark-framed glasses and nods to me as he rings up a customer's bill.

Conversations in the room resume at a dull buzz, and I sit back, crossing my arms. "If you don't want to help me, I understand. I'll get it done, or at least try. They have a skeletal staff on holidays, because everyone wants to be home with their families."

Mercury Thunder, a violin maker, walks in and adjusts his red and white polka dot bow tie, which is clipped to his long, gray beard. I wave him over, and he smiles, joining us. My dog Buddy appreciates Mercury's ear rubs and gave him a paws up, so I invited Mercury, along with a few others, to join us in making plans.

Irena Fishbone strides in and sits with us. I asked her because we'll need her boat and skippering services to pull off my plan. Next, Violet from Outrigger Services saunters in, unzips her black leather jacket and says, "Hope you didn't start without me?"

I take a deep breath, look around the group of friendly faces, and say, "I'm proposing we go to Shore Lodge tomorrow afternoon to possibly help four residents who were admitted against their will. But it's a locked ward, so this won't be a garden party. Everything in my heart tells me to go there and offer them a way out, because it's the right thing to do. Will you join me?"

Mary nods. "I'll help you."

Mercury's eyes flit to the floor before he nods, saying, "Sure."

Irena smacks the table. "I'm in."

Violet grins. "Yes."

Karina drums her fingers on the table. "You bet."

I lean in. "Thanks for agreeing to help me. We could

call this Operation Winter Storm, because the weather's about to change."

Irena nods. "Yep, the barometer's dropping. A storm's on the way."

Violet chuckles. "Not sure we need a code name, but fine."

Karina brightens. "I like it."

Mary pats my arm. "I'll help anyway I can."

I grin and raise my coffee cup. "Here's to a successful journey to Shore Lodge, and please don't tell a soul about this."

We clink mugs, and my hands tremble. Nurse Wright and her crew are formidable foes determined to keep their residents safe inside the locked unit on Cedar Island. I blow out a breath and worry about dragging my friends into trouble. A pesky thought flits past, but I brush it away. If my son Dusty knew about this he'd probably say I'm bonkers and deserve to be admitted to Shore Lodge for good for dreaming up this ill-advised scheme.

2

DUSTY

I scowl, gazing at the rundown cabin I'm renting near the mountains, and shake my head. The air inside is cold, and I can see my breath. If my mother could see me now, would she feel sorry for me and give me back my construction company?

I go outside and bring in an armful of firewood, dropping it on the floor. I dreamed up the project with Dad, so it's not fair that my mother will build Stone Estates. I picked out the plot of land, looking north to Cedar Island and west to the San Juan Islands.

Crumpling newspaper, I stuff it into a wood stove. No one will hire me in Millersville because it got out that I sold Mom's garden store and kept the money. But how many of them would've done the same in my place?

I clench my jaw and add sticks of kindling. I paid for her stay at Shore Lodge, which wasn't cheap. I acted in her best interests, so I don't see why people are bent out of shape. I should be a hero for helping my mom, but all I get are open-mouthed stares and snide comments on the streets of my hometown.

I kneel and pull out a lighter, clicking it and holding it to the newspaper, which smolders and bursts into flickering flames. I wish my life was as bright and full of promise as this little fire, but I seem to be on a downhill slide, heading for disaster.

I close the door to the wood stove and turn, tripping on a piece of wood and falling flat on my face. I miss my father and his financial support. Now that he's gone, I'm stuck in a cold cabin in the middle of nowhere.

I let out a sigh and stand up. I need to turn my life around, but I don't know how. I've never been self-sufficient because Dad always gave me money when I needed it.

I add a log to the fire, and smoke billows out, blinding me. Covering my eyes and coughing, I stumble to the door and fling it open to a chilly morning. Light mist falls, but weather forecasters are calling for snow, which is rare on our part of the Pacific Northwest. I inhale pure fresh mountain air and blow it out. I don't want to live here. I'd rather be in my apartment in Millersville, but I can't afford it anymore.

Leaning against the door jamb, I gnaw on a fingernail. My mother always invites me to Christmas Eve dinner, but she hasn't done that this year. Families should be together to celebrate the holidays. Maybe I'll just show up at her place on Christmas Eve. If she doesn't want me there, I'll be the uninvited guest souring the mood.

I grin and go back inside, reaching out and grabbing a bottle of whiskey, gulping down a slug for breakfast. Christmas Eve is her favorite holiday, and I'll give her the gift of a surprise visit.

3

JACKLYN

I drum my fingers on the table, ready to get down to specifics, and Karina comes by filling coffee cups. Violet, Mercury and Irena order quiche and scones. Resting a hand on my stomach, I say, "I'm stuffed. It was delicious, as always."

My voice is tight, because I'm asking my friends to support an idea with risks. They offered to help in any way they could after I made it home from Shore Lodge, but I fear I'm overstepping boundaries. On the dark night I ran from Shore Lodge, I promised myself I'd go back one day for the four others who were admitted unjustly by family. I must follow through, if I want to live with myself.

I cradle a cup of coffee and clear my throat, looking around the table. "I'll understand if you want to walk away from the table and don't want to help. Things could go sideways."

No one moves. I say, "We're going to enter a secure facility and leave, if all goes well, with four people. None of us are qualified for such a venture, except Violet, with your military background." I nod to her.

Violet grins at me and shrugs, in her self-deprecating, humble way. With her covert operations background, she'll help make this mission a success.

Mercury says, "I'm just the dog whisperer, and I'll watch Buddy while you're gone, but what you said about the guy whose son admitted him gave me goosebumps." He shudders. "Someone's got to do something for those people who are trapped inside and don't deserve it."

Karina slides into a seat. "I want to help, however I can."

Violet takes her hand. They were secret half-sisters but now it's out in the open, and everyone in town knows about it.

Mary blows out a breath. "I support your cause, but I'd rather not go over to the island. But if you think of anything I can do from town, I'm your gal."

I turn to Irena, who owns a boat rescue business. "Are you willing to take us on your boat? It might cause a fuss on the ferry, if we went that route."

Irena says, "Sure, I'll take you on my boat to Cedar Island, and I'll be at the dock until you come back."

I nod. "Thanks, I appreciate that. So, here's the plan. Mary and Mercury will stay on land doing what they can to help, while the rest of us will head over to the island.

Irena will drop us off and wait. Karina, Violet and I will enter Shore Lodge, and we'll gain entry posing as a singing group. If we're in luck, we'll go to the secure second floor, sing carols, and I'll talk with my friends, offering them a chance to leave and giving them the forms to revoke their power of attorney. We'll race back to the boat and take off for town. It sounds easy, but I have a feeling there'll be wrinkles along the way."

Karina bites her lower lip. "You mentioned an older gentleman who is using a wheelchair. If he wants to leave, it'll take a while to get him to the boat."

I cock my head. "I could push him in the wheelchair or carry him." I hold up my right arm and make a muscle, grinning at my friends.

Violet drums her fingers on the table. "I might be able to arrange for a helicopter."

Irena says, "The weather forecast is calling for gale force winds and gusts of fifty to sixty-five miles per hour."

Violet shakes her head. "Forget the helicopter. That's out."

Karina says, "Your orders are ready." She serves the food and sits down. "Are you sure we'll be able to sweet-talk our way in? It sounds unlikely to work."

I pick at a cuticle. "I'm in touch with someone who works there, and I think this is the best approach. But you're right, it is unlikely. The second floor is secure, and the staff is trained to turn away strangers. I'll have to convince them to let us in. Our advantage is one of surprise on the eve of a holiday, when people are distracted by personal plans and wish they were home. They'll be more likely to let us in on Christmas Eve afternoon. But it is possible that we'll go all the way over there, and no one will want to leave with us. Our mission might be a fool's errand and by tomorrow night, you'll say the idea should've been dead and buried."

Mary raises her eyebrows. "Are you done being a dark cloud? We know you can handle any emergency that comes up after what you went through at Shore Lodge."

I smile. "Thanks. I really want to do this. Are you sure you're with me?"

They set down their forks, look into my eyes and nod, saying, "Yes."

"Good," I say. "There's one last thing to consider. If my four friends come back to town with us, where will they live? They could stay at my place, but it's not a long-term solution."

Mercury says, "Leave that to me. They could bunk with me for a few months."

I clear my throat. "They'll need their medications. I'd hate for them to have medical problems without their medicine."

Mary says, "We don't want to hurt them by helping them."

Violet says, "We'll take them to the walk-in clinic when they get to town to get medications."

Mary waves a hand. "Before they go anywhere in town,

it'll be essential for me to notarize their new durable power of attorney, so their families can't admit them to Shore Lodge again."

I say, "Why don't you give me four copies, and I have them sign them there?"

Karina bites her lip. "Are you sure this is the best thing to do? It's sounds shady."

I let out a sigh. "I've been wrestling with that, but each of the four people told me they were admitted against their will to the psych ward, despite being coherent and even-keeled."

Irena nods. "I get what you're saying."

I nod. "I want to give them the respect they deserve and a choice to walk out with us or stay. We all want to be free, don't we?"

I slap my palm on the table, and silverware rattles. Diners glance over, and I wave to them, saying, "Sorry, just spouting off my opinions. Go back to your conversations, and I apologize."

Mary nudges me and says, "Let's focus on planning and issues at our own table."

I massage my aching temples and nod to my friends, who are eating. "To wrap things up, I know this is a huge undertaking, and a winter storm is on the way, but I promised myself I'd go back for them. When I was locked in there, I was the lowest I've ever been, and I don't want them to feel they've been left to wither on the vine. I appreciate you joining me on this journey. It might be dangerous, given the storm, and I'm not sure we'll gain access to the secure second floor."

My gaze flicks over my friends, measuring their commitment to the project. "Whatever you do, please don't tell anyone what we're up to." I rap the table for good luck. "Thanks everyone. We'll meet tomorrow afternoon at one o'clock at Irena's boat in the marina. Wear warm clothes, a coat and a hat. See you tomorrow."

I stand and say goodbye to each person as the group disperses, shaking hands, hugging and clapping them on the back while Mary lingers at the table. When the others have left, Mary says, "You can cancel this crazy plan. We can text everyone, drop the idea like a hot potato and stay home drinking eggnog with whisky. Doesn't that sound good? You don't have to follow through with a promise you made. No one's making you do this."

I tug on my earlobe, considering her offer of the easy way out. The notion of hanging out with her on the sofa appeals to my lazier side. But deep down, I'm driven to return to Cedar Island to free my friends, and this plan should go well, as long as Dusty doesn't get wind of it. I bet he's itching to get me admitted to Shore Lodge again, so he can take back control of Stone Construction.

I grit my teeth. I'll never forgive my son for abandoning Buddy at a shelter when I was locked inside Shore Lodge. It's a miracle Buddy and I are both alive. "I've never liked eggnog, or fruitcake for that matter, and I won't back down, or I couldn't live with myself. We're going ahead."

She shrugs. "Thought I'd give you a last chance to drop it." She glances at my khaki shorts and mismatched socks. "Aren't you cold?"

I slap cash on the table and smile, walking with her to the door. "I'm fine." As we leave, I wave to my Bernard, who is clearing tables.

Going to our cars, Mary glances at my hiking boots. "You might want to wear running shoes tomorrow."

"I'll think about it, but they have good traction, and they've gotten me through tough scrapes."

We stop by my car, and she holds my gaze. "Why did you invite Mercury to our meeting? He doesn't appear to have special skills, like the rest of us."

I chuckle. "He'll watch Buddy while I'm gone, and I'm enjoying his company. Karina's skill could be mesmerizing the psych ward staff with hot coffee and scones."

She jabs a finger at me. "That's brilliant. Have her bring scones, quiche and hot coffee to bribe your way into Shore Lodge and get upstairs."

A wide smile spreads across my face. "Perfect, I'll go ask her."

"I'll pay for it."

I shake my head. While I've been happy and playing with my loveable dog, those at Shore Lodge are shut inside. "My guilt about leaving them behind is driving this project, so I'll cover the cost. Do you think we should ask Fred to come along and act as an attorney?"

"He tells people he doesn't give out free advice, and he

might try to talk you out of it. And I'm glad you're making friends with someone as kind as Mercury seems."

We hug each other and say goodbye, and I go into the café to talk to Karina. Striding up to the counter, I imagine her bribing the staff at Shore Lodge with food. If we pull this off, my guilt about being free will scuttle away like a cloud pushed by high winds.

I say to Bernard, "Okay if I go in the back? I need to speak to Karina."

He says, "Is this about the secret project? The one I'm not supposed to know about?"

I roll my eyes. There are no secrets in this small town. "Did she tell you?"

He shakes his head. "No, I was clearing tables and happened to hear a few details about Shore Lodge and the second floor. You're pulling some people out, is that right?"

I put my hands together and practically beg. "Please, don't tell anyone. We don't need a crowd of looky-loos, or people stopping us."

"I won't," he says, adjusting his black-framed glasses. "You can trust me."

I don't say it, but I doubt anyone in town can keep a secret longer than two seconds. My hands shake as I walk to the kitchen in back. I just want to survive the next two days and help the folks in Shore Lodge who wanted to be whisked away.

4

DUSTY

I lock up the cabin and jump in my truck, driving down a rutted dirt road to the tiny town of Foothills, Washington, population eight-hundred people. Living near the North Cascades mountains, I could be planning a snow-shoeing trip with friends, but my buddies have ghosted me. If they knew how I grew up, they'd understand my side of the story.

I shake my head at how it was always Rose this and Rose that. At the dinner table, my parents gushed about my sister's accomplishments and blathered on about their garden store. I'd gulp down food and run to my room. I was the unseen child, and so that's why I figure I deserved to take an early inheritance when I sold Mom's store.

I roll down the window, feeling cold air whip against my cheeks. Moving wasn't really my choice, but after being socially frozen out of Millersville, I had to go. Plus, I couldn't afford my apartment anymore. When I'm on my way up and back in my hometown, those who shunned me will turn on the roasting spit of shame, burning with regret for how they treated me.

My mouth waters, picturing eating barbeque chicken, and I rub my rumbling stomach. A mountain looms over the small town where I don't belong. Foothills isn't next to a big body of water near the San Juan Islands, like Millersville. Instead, I'm marooned where an avalanche could tumble down, covering my cabin.

I pull off the road and climb out for a better look. Crossing my arms and staring at snow-covered Mt. Shuksan to the north, I vow to be more like this mountain, withstanding forces trying to wear it down. A shiver runs up my spine. I'll be mountain-tough, shrugging off glares, and ignore my mother's cold shoulder. I'll survive and be there when the snow melts and spring arrives.

Cold seeps into my bones, wafting over from a river cutting through town. My parents used to take my sister and me camping near here when we were little, before they spent all their time at their garden store. The smell of grilled steak drifts through the air, and my stomach growls. A ray of hope flares at the spark of an idea. If I stop by today, Mom might invite me in for lunch, and we'll patch things up. Maybe she'll give me a check for Christmas, like she used to.

I hop in my truck, jot down a quick poem in a notebook and drive, patting my pockets and pulling out a cigarette and lighter. Lighting up as I head down the road, I consider my situation. My bank account is bone dry, and although I should find a job, I don't want to work for someone else. I want to run my own construction company. If I wear Mom down enough, maybe she'll cave and give my company back. If she won't, I'll have to mull over the idea of ushering her to the final end to her life, to benefit mine.

I drive past an old cement factory, which some say is haunted. Ghost hunters have gotten hurt there, and the building is off-limits to the public. But rules don't apply to me, so I'll stop and explore it another time. Today I'll swing by Mom's place. If she refuses to let me in, I'll back up in the driveway, rev the engine and let smoke billow toward the house. That'll teach her to treat me right.

Wiping a tear from my eye, I wish my father was alive. He understood how money flowed like water through my bank account, and he supported me. When I was in fourth grade and got caught stealing candy at the corner store, he hurried over, talked to the owner, paid for the chocolate bar and apologized for me. He told me not to tell Mom, which I never did, and after that, I knew Dad had my back no matter what I did.

I take a deep drag from my cigarette and grip the steering wheel, making a turn. Tomorrow night, I'll sit at

Mom's table for her special Christmas Eve dinner. She'll come to her senses and beg me to come work for her as foreman.

Tapping my brakes at a stop light, I recall seeing her after she returned from Shore Lodge. I overheard her say to friends, "Katie bar the door," when she saw me. That's right, mother dear, a fight's about to break out, and you'd better get ready, because I'm coming for Christmas Eve dinner, whether you like it or not. I deserve to be there. Maybe I'll spend the night in my old bedroom.

I smile. That would bug her. I'll make myself at home as a bargaining chip, so she'll give me back my company. A streak of stubbornness is called for, and I know who I inherited that trait from.

I head west on Highway 20 for Millersville. Watch out, Mom, I'm coming over to celebrate the holiday with you, like we did with Dad. Get my room ready, because I'll be crashing there, and I expect to be served home-cooked meals. I'll be the uninvited guest stirring things up, making you nervous, and it won't be long before you see things my way and give me back Stone Construction.

But as I approach Mom's house, the lights are off, her car is gone and it looks like nobody is home. I glance around but don't see nosy neighbors peering through parted curtains, so I slide off my ripped truck seat. I'll take a look around to see how she redid the place after I gave it a facelift.

Tossing my cigarette butt on the front lawn, just to bug her when she sees it, I ease my way around back to look in the windows. Her dog barks, yips and whines, scratching at the back door. I say, "Buddy, it's me. It's all good. Don't worry about it."

I pull out my house key and stick it in the lock, but it doesn't slide in. I frown and try it again, jiggling it back and forth. Buddy barks and growls. She must have changed the locks. What kind of mother would do that to her own flesh and blood?

I hear heavy footsteps come around the outside of the house, and a man says, "Hello?"

Bernard Frackus, my high school science teacher stops when he sees me. "What're you doing here?"

I open my palms. "Mom asked me to check her toilet and said it's running."

He tilts his head and touches his glasses. "She didn't mention that, and I just saw her. What're you really doing here?"

I gesture to the door, where Buddy whines. "She also wants me to let Buddy out. I guess he needs a walk, and she's busy."

He nods. "She was headed to the grocery store to get supplies."

I cross my arms. "For her Christmas Eve dinner, like she does?"

He glances away, staring at a broadleaf maple tree. When I was young, my parents drilled into me the names and types of trees they sold at the garden store, so I could help out and maybe own it one day. But that didn't interest me. I wanted to build things instead, glorious structures to house people's dreams for their futures.

Mr. Frackus says, "No, I think she's got other plans for tomorrow."

My eyebrows go up. "She always has a big turkey on Christmas Eve, every year. What's so important she'd miss it?"

"Can't say. You'll have to ask her. Now if you'll excuse me, I've got to get some groceries out of the car and into the fridge."

The dog barks, and I stare at the back door, wanting to break it down. One big kick or two is all it would take. But then I think about what my retired science teacher said. My mother is working on something, and it sounds like a secret project. I'd better get going before she sees me and suspects I'm watching her.

I trot to my truck, start it up and go down the street, parking under a tree and paging through a notebook with my poems. I clear my throat and read aloud a poem I wrote on the way here when I stopped by the side of the road.

"Snowy mountain, sure of yourself, make me strong and steady.

Despite everyone hating me, I want to be majestic like you.

A winter storm is coming, but you won't be moved.

Make me tall and mighty as a mountain. Let me be loved again."

I wipe tears from my eyes, set the poem aside and pull binoculars for bird watching from the glove compartment. Training them on the house where I grew up, I say, "What're you up to, Mom? I'll find out."

5

JACKLYN

Driving home, I pass what looks like my son's mud-splattered white truck parked down the block. The driver hunkers down in the seat and turns away. My son is a big, broad-shouldered man, and the sight of him trying to hide in plain sight strikes me as funny. I chuckle and tap the horn, just to see what he'll do, but he doesn't look up.

I park in the driveway and glance in the back seat. I have extra blankets, in case we'll need them tomorrow after our boat trip, and food, which I unload and haul into the kitchen. I let Buddy out in the yard, and he chases a crow. The bird flies off and comes swooping down. Buddy gives chase, and the crow flaps away. I smile at my sweet dog, who is sitting and panting, and go in the house. I have much to do before we meet at the boat tomorrow.

In what had been my son's bedroom when he was growing up, I set up a camp bed I slept on a few months ago after I swam in frigid water and nearly met my death in Cedar Channel. I open the closet and nod at a blow-up mattress and spare pillows. I'm as ready as I'll ever be for overnight guests, if a few residents leave Shore Lodge with us.

Buddy runs in the yard, ears flapping, and I bite my lower lip. My grand idea may be misguided, and the timing means I won't be home preparing Christmas Eve dinner, which is one of my favorite times of the year, gathered around a candle-lit table sharing good food, stories and laughter. But I promised myself that when I got out, I'd go back and give the others a chance at freedom.

Standing by the front window, I pick up the phone and call my daughter. My son drives by, and his truck backfires. I flinch and grit my teeth, because if he thinks he can intimidate me and wrest back control of Stone Construction, he's wasting his time.

Rose picks up and says, "I was just about to call you. Are you having people over for Christmas Eve, like you always do?"

I hesitate, not wanting to say too much, and I don't want her telling her brother about my plans. It would be like him out of spite to find a way to interfere. "This year I'm doing something a little different."

"What's that? Going to Uncle Fred's and Aunt Mary's for dinner?"

"I'm going on a boat ride."

"Have a great time. We just walked in the door. I've got to go."

"Love you," I say, but she's already hung up.

6

NURSE WRIGHT

The next morning at home, Nurse Wright rubbed salt on a prime rib and pushed the pan in a hot oven. She smiled. By the time her guests arrived, the roast would be ready to serve. She put whole cranberries in a blender with orange rind and hummed "Jingle Bells." The tune had been running through her mind ever since yesterday's caroling activity at work.

She looked in the living room, where the long dining table was set with red placemats, tall green candles in glass candlesticks and fresh cut fir boughs. Her husband had done that part. She added sugar to the cranberry relish and plopped it in a bowl, setting it in the refrigerator to chill. Her Christmas Eve dinner was coming together.

She pursed her lips, because by the time she arrived at

the grocery store in Millersville last night, the best turkeys were sold out. The only ones left were too small to feed her guests or too large to fit in her oven. But there were far worse problems in the world than having to settle for prime rib, and she knew they were fortunate to live on a beautiful island. Her high-paying job, which few wanted because it involved working in a secure psychiatric ward on an isolated island, meant she could afford to buy whatever food they wanted.

Her husband poured a cup of coffee and sat at the breakfast bar. "Need some help? I can make the cranberry sauce."

"Thanks, but it's done. I have a certain way of making it, and I'd rather do it myself."

He nodded. "That's why you're good at your job. Everything has to be just right."

She tilted her head. "Some might say I'm a control freak, but I just like things done my way."

He arched an eyebrow and reached for his mug. Her phone rang, and she groaned, grabbing a paper towel and wiping her hands. She was taking today and tomorrow off, but it might be about an emergency at work. Her pulse picked up, and she answered. "Hello?"

"I'm sorry to bother you, Nurse Wright," a young woman said in a shaking voice, "but Florence isn't feeling well, and she threw up. Should I send her to the infirmary?"

Nurse Wright tightened her grip on the phone. This

was not a reason to call the boss on a day off. "Does she have a fever?"

"I didn't check. Hold on."

Nurse Wright rolled her eyes and waited.

Her husband said, "Do you have to go in? Last year, it ruined our special dinner."

She said, "I'll tell them not to call again unless there's an emergency."

The nurse at Shore Lodge came on the line. "No, her temperature isn't elevated."

"Then it must be something she ate. There is a stomach bug going around. Keep her in her room and force fluids. Don't let her get dehydrated. And yes, if she throws up again, take her down to the infirmary. But please, don't call me again today or tomorrow unless it is an absolute emergency. Do you understand?"

After a beat of silence, the nurse said, "I understand."

7

IRENA

I drive my boat in the morning through the marina to the fuel dock and tie up, nodding to a young guy with curly dark hair who works there. He waves from behind the counter. I'm a frequent customer, as owner of Nimbus Boat Rescue.

Heavy mist falls as I unscrew the fuel cap on the boat deck, shove in the nozzle and squeeze the handle, sniffing the air. The smell of diesel brings a smile to my face, because I love how I make my living. Going to the rescue of boaters in distress pays my bills and fills me with meaning and purpose.

A seagull flies overhead, flapping its wings, fighting the wind, and I chew on the inside of my mouth. I don't offer my boat services for free to friends, but Jacklyn has been through so much, with her husband passing away, leaving her unpaid medical bills and her son admitting her to Shore Lodge, that my heart goes out to her, and I want to help. I just hope our mission this afternoon will go smoothly, despite the bleak weather forecast of high winds and small craft warnings.

I glance beyond the breakwater to the choppy bay, where white caps are kicking up, and blow out a breath as worried thoughts race through my mind. Could I get in trouble and be slapped with a fine because I helped with Jacklyn's plan? If I can't pay the penalty, would the authorities take my boat?

I grip the nozzle, listening to the whoosh of fuel filling the tanks, and vow to make Jacklyn's venture work out because I can't risk losing my boat business if we're arrested. My daughter needs her mother out of jail, a roof over her head, healthy food and dance lessons to be happy, and I want to be the best mother Kelly could have.

Wind whips past, pulling strands of hair from my ponytail and into my eyes. I've waited ten years for my ex to pay child support, but I'm last in line to be paid by Jack and his new wife Abby. At least they promised to pay me back, when he's recovered from his head injury and trained in a new line of work.

A dented white truck drives past, back firing and stopping at nearby Seafarers' Park, and Jacklyn's son Dusty climbs out. We know each other from growing up in the same small town. He's ten years younger than me and strikes me as having a chip on his shoulder and someone who excels in looking out for themselves first and foremost. I hope he won't see me and come over, asking about his mother.

He glances out toward the bay and turns my way. I avert my eyes and focus on the amount of fuel going into my boat. The numbers are ticking by, adding up fast. This will be an expensive Christmas Eve jaunt. If she tries to pay me, I'll refuse to take her money. She's part of our found family group, so of course I'll help her.

I steal a furtive glance at Dusty, and he nods, walking toward the fuel dock. I shouldn't have looked over. I know Jacklyn wouldn't want me talking to him and risking people finding out what we're up to today. She deserves a medal for courage and the Amazing Woman of the Year award.

Fuel rushes through the hose as Dusty thuds down the ramp. He's wearing a black and white checked flannel shirt with worn jeans, and he's tall. His boots are big, and his stride is heavy, leaving a trail of caked dirt behind him with each step. He approaches and shoves his hands in his pockets. "Hey, Irena."

I nod, acting like I have nothing to hide. "Hey."

He glances at the boat and says, "Nice boat."

"Thanks."

"Whatcha doing out here today?"

A stiff breeze brushes past my cheeks. He's standing close, and the hairs on my neck stand on end. I check the numbers on the fuel pump. In only a few more minutes, I'll be finished and hop in my boat. If he watches me in the marina, I won't return to my slip, because I don't want him to see his mother board my boat. If that happens, I'll take a quick spin around the bay to distract him.

"Re-fueling," I say. "Got to be ready for when a distress call comes in."

He crosses his arms and leans in, so close I smell cigarettes and a hint of booze on his breath. "Are you doing something with my mother later today?"

I tighten my grip on the nozzle, willing the fuel to finish filling the tanks, and say, "I thought your family had Christmas Eve dinner together each year?"

He frowns and rubs his cheek, turning to stare at a red-hulled transport boat running supplies to a tanker anchored out in the bay. "Not this year. My mom and I aren't getting along. She's riled up about the favor I did for her, putting her in Shore Lodge."

I break out coughing. What gall he has to act like his admitting her to a secure psychiatric unit when she was of sound mind was the right thing to do. I want to kick him in the shins, but I say, "Not everyone sees it that way."

He grunts. "She forgot her own name at the doctor's office. It was that bad. There are two sides to every story, and people have only heard hers. It's not fair how the whole town turned against me."

The fuel shuts off. I set the nozzle in the holder and look him in the eye. "Hate to tell you, but I'm on your mom's side. It wasn't right what you did, selling her store out from under her and locking her up so you could take her money. You were about to sell her house. And poor Buddy, you left him at the shelter. Do you have no decency? Who would do that to such a sweet dog?"

He scuffs a toe. "My dad would've wanted me to go ahead with Stone Estates, no matter what the cost, so that's why I did it."

I point at his chest. "Really? Wake up. You were all in for yourself. You ripped off a grieving widow when she was most vulnerable. I'd say you're number one in your book, that's for sure."

He shrugs, glances at what I owe for fuel and whistles. "Man, that's a lot." He opens his hand. "Do you have fifty bucks you can lend me? I'm broke and hungry, and I need to get gas."

I snort. "Nope, sorry, I can't. Go find a job."

He shoves his hands in his jeans pockets. "No one will hire me because of Mom bad-mouthing me. She made up stories, but I did what I thought was best for her."

I roll my eyes. He's more deluded than I suspected. "You better come down to earth and accept reality or move to where no one's heard the story. Maybe start over in Idaho. Everyone's moving there. Make a fresh start."

He rubs his cheek. "I don't want to start over. I want what I had back."

I shrug. "When we don't want change, sometimes it's forced on us. See you around."

I step inside to pay for fuel and hope that's the last I'll see of Dusty for a long time.

8

JACKLYN

I pace in the living room while Buddy watches with concern. My new friend Mercury jumps up from the couch and says, "I'll make a fresh pot of coffee. That might help while you're waiting to go."

I stop and rub Buddy's ears, saying, "Thanks, I'm so nervous about this afternoon, I'm about to jump out of my skin."

I glance outside at a misty morning, recalling something my husband Albert said years ago when Mary and I went kayaking. *Be safe and stay alive.*

I waved on my way out, leaving him with our young kids. My fingers tingled, I was beyond ready to slip away from family and spend a quiet day on the water with a friend. I said, "Call Fred or Bernice if you need help. We'll be back when we can. We're putting in at the Washington Park boat launch by the big old tree."

Albert furrowed his brow and rushed over, wrapping his arms around me. Dusty and Rose, left on a blanket spread on the carpet, started to cry and held out their little arms to me. He said, "Be safe and stay alive. Come back to us. The current's strong today."

Laughing, I said, "But we're strong and mighty. Nothing will stop us."

Mary and I laughed as she drove to the park, and we launched our kayaks, paddling away from the boat launch and hugging Fidalgo Island's shoreline. All was easy on a beautiful sunny day until the currents grew stronger and the wind picked up, pushing us north toward Cypress Island.

Mary yelled in a frantic voice, "I'm not sure I can do this. My arms are tired."

"Dig in," I called, sea spray splashing my face, "give it all you've got. We can do this."

I stayed as close to her as I could and we dipped and paddled, backs straining, hands growing numb from the chill of the water and the wind. "Come on, Mary, we can do this. We'll get home."

She clenched her jaw and said in a loud voice, "You're right, we can do this. We'll get home."

I echoed her all the way back to the boat launch, and with each paddle stroke, Mary and I chanted, "We'll get home."

We stepped out of the water on shaky legs, put the kayaks on top of her car and slumped into the seats, exhausted. I turned to her and grinned. "Ready to do it all over again?"

She patted my knee. "We're lucky we made it back alive. This is it for me. Tomorrow I'll sell my kayak. Thanks for your help out there. If not for you, I might have overturned and be fish food on the bottom of the Salish Sea."

"Anything for you," I said.

She gave me a weak smile. "Same back."

Now, Albert's words spool through my mind in a cautionary refrain. Be safe and stay alive. That's what we've got to do on our adventure to Cedar Island.

I follow Mercury and sit down at the kitchen table while he works. Buddy comes over, nuzzling me. I run a hand over his silky ears, saying, "I hope I'm not making a mistake today. I never wanted to go back before this because I was afraid they'd trap me again." A shudder runs through me, and I pat Buddy's chest, murmuring, "Good dog."

Mercury fills the coffee pot with tap water.

I say, "I can't tell you how awful it was to be locked inside that place. I hate tight confined spaces, and I felt like I couldn't breathe when I was there. Not to mention what happened in the basement, but that's a story for another time."

Mercury nods and grinds the coffee beans and pushes a button to start the coffee brewing and wipes his hands on a towel before coming over and sitting down. He takes my hand and says, "This is something you feel you must do, and I respect that. We'll help you anyway we can. Run away as fast as you can if it turns bad when you get inside."

I nod. "The closer we get to going, the more the idea feels absurd. Why in the name of all sanity would I return to a place where I suffered so much? But Florence and the others were envious of my plans to escape, and I want to give them the same chance."

He sits back and says, "You've got a case of pre-recital jitters. I hope this coffee will be as good as Karina makes it at the café. She showed me a trick to try."

"What's that?"

"Add a few drops of water when grinding the beans for best results."

I smile. "I'd like to add a splash of whiskey and sit back and relax, but we're due to leave soon. I've got to carry through and do what I think is best for them."

Mercury cocks his head and tugs on his long gray beard. "Funny how that works, isn't it? You see it as the right thing to do, but their families apparently don't agree."

I blow out a breath. "We'll know by tonight whether it was worth it. Maybe the answer lies in the gray space, where everyone holds a different view and no one's right."

"Except their doctors. We have to respect that."

I thump the table with a fist. "But four people were admitted to a warehouse of souls without their permission, and they're smart. They can talk and feed themselves, and they know what's going on. I can't let it rest until I see them."

"They're lucky you're in their court. Do you have the forms Mary brought by?"

I touch my pocket. "Yes, they're right here, along with the Fran's Park Bar you gave me." Buddy sits by the treat jar, staring at me, and I say, "If we're late getting back, remember to give Buddy his first and second dinners."

He nods. "I'll do that, and don't worry. Everything on land will be fine. It's the sea part that bothers me, but I bet you'll all be fine."

I open my hands. "I hope we'll bring some of them home. By the way, my son has been creeping around the house, so be ready if he stops by. He's angry at me, and you'll have to stand up to him."

He smooths his mustache. "No problem. I've been wanting to meet your son anyway. Don't worry, I'll protect your place and your pup. You just get home to Buddy and me in one piece."

I step into his open arms and lean into a hug, absorbing his warmth. A branch scratches against the house, and a gust of wind rattles the window panes. As I pat Mercury's back, Buddy rubs against my leg. He's my emotional barometer and knows I'm jittery about my upcoming journey. Every cell in my body is screaming for me to hop on Irena's boat, get the job done and come home, where we'll be safe from the oncoming winter storm.

I bend and look into Buddy's brown eyes, patting his chest. "Don't worry, sweet pup, I'll be home soon."

9

———

VIOLET

I gather my team at Outrigger Services, and we sit in the bull pen. "I know today is Christmas Eve, but we've got work to do. I'll be heading out on Irena Fishbone's boat soon, and I'd like you guys to be here, in case anything goes wrong."

Mimi pulls her hair back in a pony tail. "What's the plan? Give us the details."

Vince checks his watch. "Sorry, but I have a hard stop at three this afternoon. I've got to be home early for the baby's first Christmas Eve. Tonight's a big deal for my wife."

Mimi says, "Go home, we'll cover it."

He nods. "I appreciate that."

Flora says in her high-pitched voice, "What's the plan? Tell us where we're needed."

I clear my throat. "Don't tell anyone outside this room, but a small group of us are going over to Shore Lodge on Cedar Island early this afternoon. Jacklyn Stone wants to see if we can break out a few residents from the locked psych ward. She says they're of sound mind, but their families admitted them. Sounds pretty cold and hard-hearted, doesn't it?"

They nod, and Vince grips the arms of a chair, veins in his hands standing out. It must really bother the big guy. I review the plan and say, "Flora, why don't you monitor the police scanner, see what they're saying and let me know if anyone reports a break in at Shore Lodge. Keep an eye on socials and chat rooms for postings. We don't want throngs of people jumping in boats and coming over, or making things difficult by getting in the way. The plan is pretty impossible, as it stands, and we'll need luck on our side to enter the building, extract four people, if they're willing to go, and get back to town without serious injuries."

Flora cringes. "Sounds risky."

"It might be, or it could go as easy as eating apple pie."

Vince grins. "I'll have my piece with a slice of cheddar cheese."

Mimi scoffs. "No way. I'll take mine with a scoop of vanilla ice cream."

I cut off the banter by saying, "Mimi, I'd like you to be ready to run down to the marina, in case we come in hot to the dock and need help. If the police try to arrest us, work your magic with the Police Chief. They liked us pretty well after we helped quell riots when 'trouble came to town' or the 'fiasco on Fidalgo,' as the press called it."

I wipe my palms on my pants. "Any questions?"

They shake their heads. "Good luck, boss."

10

KARINA

I cover slices of quiche with tin foil, and a tear dribbles down my cheek, recalling my grand-mother and the cooking she did when I was growing up in the café. When she was on her death bed, I promised her I'd move home from Seattle, run her café and read her diary. Her journal was stolen, but when I tracked it down and perused the pages, the secrets buried there ripped apart my illusions of the quiet family I thought we had.

I wipe tears from my face and let out a sigh. My grand-mother made this job look easy, but since she died, I've been running all the time. It took me a while to get my sea legs, as Irena might say given her preference for maritime references, but I'm managing the restaurant and making art now without it feeling like a juggling act.

I cross my arms, eying the thermos I set out for coffee.

Bernard Frackus comes in the kitchen and says, "Something on your mind?"

I had no idea he was dating my grandmother until I read her diary, and my jaw dropped when I read what she wrote. I thought I knew my grandmother well, but reading her journal let me into her life on a whole new level.

I tap my lips. "If you worked in a psych unit, would you rather have individual cups of coffee to tempt you or a thermos full?"

"Both," he says, fiddling with his black-framed glasses. "Bring empty cups. Pour coffee from the thermos, so the aroma wafts out. That'll entice them to open the door. Do you have the scones ready?"

"Yep. And I'm not bringing jam. It'd be too sticky. I don't want to leave jam fingerprints behind when we run out."

"Very funny," he says. "Be careful out there. I want you to come back safe and sound. Gigi would take me to an early grave if she knew I was letting you take these risks."

I smile because he's my new favorite fake grandfather. "I'm glad you care enough to worry about me. We'll focus on offering the sane people a way out, and we'll be fine. See you later."

"Dinner tomorrow, at my place?"

"Let's we have Christmas dinner here, in the café instead? If Gigi were with us, she'd want that."

"Tomorrow it is, and check in when you get home. Let me know how it goes."

"I will. It helps that my sister, the expert in all things impossible, will be there."

He gives me a quick hug. "Say hi to Violet for me. Take care."

I grab a basket lined with a red and white checked cloth and load it with the thermos, quiche, scones, coffee cups, red paper napkins and plastic forks and knives. Picking up the basket, I say, "See you tomorrow, and thanks for closing up."

I walk outside, and my stomach knots. I acted tough, but in truth I'd rather sit home by the fire with my sister than go out on a boat in windy weather. But I agreed to go with the group, so I'll keep my word.

Rain drizzles down as I unlock the car and set the basket inside. Sliding behind the wheel, I take a deep breath, start the car and know my dear, departed grandmother would frown and scold me ten ways to Sunday if she knew what I was about to do.

I drive away and say aloud, "Sorry, Gigi, I know it's risky, but I've got to follow my heart and do what I feel is right."

11

IRENA

Dusty stomps away from the fuel dock, and I hop on my boat and start the engine. While it warms up, I study him from my wheelhouse. He climbs in his truck, staring out at the choppy bay, before turning to watch my boat. My hands form fists, and I look away, shaking my head. His watching me makes it too risky to return to my marina slip, where he might find his mother waiting and pester us with questions about where we're headed.

Glancing at the temperature gauge, I see the engine's warmed up and ready to go. I go out on deck, pull the dock lines onboard and drive away past the breakwater into the bay. This decoy run should distract him and put him off our true purpose.

I check the brass wall clock for the time and nod. I've got fifty-five minutes before Jacklyn is due to meet me at my slip, so I'll be fine. I frown at a sailboat washed ashore in a recent windstorm. Gale force winds roared through a week ago, howling and wailing, and the boat dragged anchor. The sailboat leans against the rocks, bumping and thumping with the rhythm of the waves, the hull tipped on its side, vulnerable to the next incoming storm.

Puttering past a viewpoint on the bluff, I wave to someone standing by a green park bench and round the point, turning into the wind and heading north into Fidalgo Bay to see how weather looks. As skipper, I'm responsible for my crew, so I want a firsthand view of the conditions before letting my friends hop onboard and venturing out.

I push the throttle down to fly over the waves, thumping over white caps and heading toward Cedar Island to scout out a hidden little dock. To the east, Jackson Bridge pulls my attention, and I glance over that way and sigh. The bridge connects two landmasses, allowing cars to move from island to island, but it has caused me and my friends much heartache. My ex-husband Jack went missing near the bridge, after he and I were swept overboard by a rogue wave from a friend's boat, and I lost a former love there too.

I shake my head to clear my thoughts and round Heron Point, skimming the waves and turning into Cedar Channel. The current is running east, and a stiff breeze is blowing. I turn toward a small private dock on Cedar Island and frown.

The dock is full, with skiffs and powerboats tied up, so I'll have to raft up to another boat when I drop Jacklyn and her team off to run ashore. My gaze turns to Shore Lodge, sitting a half-mile back from shore. The two-story building looms over a wild meadow, where squat shrubs quiver and evergreen trees sway in the wind.

A chill runs up my spine. The place may look peaceful from here, but the windows are locked and the second-floor is secure, requiring badge access. For Jacklyn, it was hell on earth. For others who have dementia, it's a fine spot to live out their days.

I turn the wheel, swing the boat around and head back to the marina. What were one-foot waves on the way out have become two-foot white caps. Jacklyn will need a lot of luck to pull this off, because sweet-talking will only take them so far. From what Jacklyn told me about her time in Shore Lodge, the head nurse, Nurse Wright, runs a tight ship.

My phone rings, and it's my thirteen-year-old daughter. I answer and say, "Hey, hon. What's going on?"

She says, "When are you coming home?"

"I'm not sure. We haven't left yet, and I don't know how long it'll take."

"What'll I eat? We usually have Christmas Eve dinner with Dad, Buzz, Abby and Craig."

I swallow a lump in my throat, because our friend Buzz is gone forever. Craig is headed to jail and blames the rest of us for what happened to him. "You know that's not happening this year. But there's food in the fridge. Eat something, and I'll be back when I can."

"Why don't you stay home and let someone else do it? You don't have to be the hero."

I smile, because my daughter knows me so well, and shrug. "I guess that's just the way I'm built. I'm wired to rescue people, and Jacklyn needs a boat to pull this off." I pass two oil refineries and turn toward the marina.

Kelly says, "Stay home. Don't go."

I shake my head. "Sorry, but no one else could do this."

"Dusty has a boat. He could take his mom over."

"Their relationship isn't on the best terms right now, so it's not an option to ask Dusty to help. Besides, he's the one who put his mom in Shore Lodge in the first place. Listen, I've got to go. I'm heading into the marina. I'll call you when I'm on the way home, but it might be late. Why don't you invite a friend over to play board games and drink eggnog?"

"Board games are boring, but I'll think about it."

"Go hang out with your dad and Abby."

"They were into spending their first Christmas Eve together, and I'd feel like I was crashing their party."

"Give him a call. Go see them. You're always welcome at their house. Do you want me to call Abby and set it up?"

"No, Mom, I'm old enough to do it myself. I'll think about it. Love you."

"Love you."

I hang up and wish I wasn't leaving my teenage daughter home alone on a holiday afternoon. In the past, I played Christmas carols while we sat by the fire drinking hot chocolate. Instead, I'm about to head out with a boat load of well-intentioned people. Violet will be there, and she's ex-military, so she knows what she's doing. But I suspect it'll take more than a gift basket of scones to get in and out safely from a locked psychiatric ward.

JACKLYN

Wind whips past as I pace by Irena's empty boat slip in the marina, and I shiver in my puffer jacket. My red long underwear worn under my khaki shorts keeps my legs warm, while adding a festive touch for the holidays. I tug my black wool watch cap down over my ears, glance over at Seafarers' Memorial Park, and my jaw drops when I see my son's beat up white truck there, facing the bay.

I walk down the dock and hope he doesn't see me. If he comes over to ask what I'm doing, his pesky probing could delay our careful plans. I suspect he'd take great delight in defeating whatever cause I'm backing, to get revenge for my taking over his company.

Wind howls and moan and whistles through the marina, making halyards rattle and clang. Pulling off our plan will be challenging with nature throwing up obstacles. I stop behind a yacht and peer around the polished white fiberglass hull toward the park as Dusty drives away.

I shiver, rubbing my arms and pacing back and forth by Irena's boat slip, and I'm reminded of my son's cruelty when I was in Shore Lodge. I swear, if Dusty was a plant, he'd be poison ivy, because brushing up against him brings agony. What a rotten world it is when I can't trust my own son.

I squint into the wind, scanning the water for Irena's boat, and reflect that I probably should have taken Dusty to a child psychologist when he was in second grade and he smeared toothpaste on the classroom windows during recess. He also cut off a girl's ponytail in class, but we thought he'd grow out of it. I sigh, weighed down by the burden of blame that rests heavy on my shoulders. But it's not all our fault as his parents. Something made Dusty who he is, coming from within, despite our best efforts.

I put my hands on my hips, staring at the marina breakwater and wishing Irena would magically appear. I'm early, but I couldn't just stay home and wait. I fiddle with my fingers in my red knit gloves. We've got to get this party started before I fly away like a dandelion in the wind.

Irena's boat plows through the water, heading my way. She slows down, putters past the breakwater and docks like a pro, hopping off the boat and tying the dock lines before I can help her. She wraps me in a hug and says, "The boat's fueled up, and we're as ready as we'll ever be."

"Thanks for doing this. I owe you. What's the weather like out in the bay?"

She shakes her head. "You don't owe me a thing. The wind's kicking up with one to two-foot chop, which shouldn't be a problem. But you look pale, like you saw a ghost."

I shudder. "I saw Dusty just now, but I don't think he saw me. That was a close call."

She shrugs. "Forget about him. I saw him at the fuel dock and didn't say a word."

I say in a tight voice, "Am I seriously out of my mind to ask you to do this?"

"Listen, even if no one at Shore Lodge leaves with you, it'll be worth it." She smiles. "But, yeah, it is a little crazy, on the eve of a holiday no less.

I let out a nervous laugh. "I hope it'll go well."

"Hey," Irena says with a kind smile, patting my back, "We've got this. We want to help you."

I blow out a breath. "It's nice to know I'm not muzzy in the head, like Dusty said. We'll sneak in and weed them out."

Irena grins, raising a fist in the air. "To our motley crew of would-be rescuers."

I mimic her gesture and flash a smile, feeling grateful

for her energy and positive attitude. I picked the right people to accompany me across the water into what for me was a barren tomb of doom. "We'll free the four who are locked inside," I say, pumping my fist. "Here's to our success."

13

IRENA

I go around giving my boat a last look and check that all is shipshape before we head to Cedar Island. The engine hums with a throaty purr, and my muscles tense as a gust of wind buffets the boat. The mist has turned to rain pattering on the boat deck. An eighteen-mile-an hour wind is blowing from the north, with stiffer winds in store for this afternoon. Beyond the marina breakwater, the sea is choppy. It'll be a rough ride, fighting the current and wind on the way to Shore Lodge.

I duck inside the boat, where Jacklyn is furiously texting someone, and glance at a brass barometer on the wall. The barometer is dropping, the wind is picking up and the boat tugs on her lines. I sigh because I'd rather be home with my daughter, sitting by the fire.

I nod at the engine temperature gage and say, "We're ready to go."

Jacklyn chews on a fingernail and checks her phone. The sooner we get this done, and I'm home, the better. I scan the dock, but don't see Violet or Karina.

I say, "What're Mercury and Mary up to?"

Jacklyn pockets her phone. "Mercury's staying with Buddy. He needs his dinners."

I smile. "Who needs his dinners?"

She chuckles. "I was talking about Buddy. Mary's home printing out durable power of attorney forms, so we'll be ready for people to revoke their old power of attorney and assign new ones. She's a notary, that's why I included her."

A call comes over the marine radio, and I step to the helm to listen. The Coast Guard is asking boats in the vicinity of Jackson Bridge to assist a sixteen-foot powerboat that ran out of fuel. I swallow and smother my initial instinct to pick up the microphone and call in, saying I'll help. Jacklyn is counting on me, and we don't have time to take a detour, going on a rescue call, although that's my business.

Jacklyn says, "Everything okay? You look worried."

I shrug. "A boat ran out of fuel. It feels uncomfortable not going to help."

"I know this is how you make your living, and I don't want to take advantage of you. Let me pay you for fuel and your time."

I swat away the suggestion with my hand. "Definitely not. You're like family to us, and I won't let you pay. After what you went through, you deserve all the help we can give."

She purses her lips. "If you insist. And thanks very much. I appreciate it."

The marine radio erupts with chatter. Someone volunteers to tow the stranded boat to the fuel dock. I smile at Jacklyn and say, "There, I don't always have to run to the rescue, do I? Others will step in."

She nods. "We don't have to be super women all the time. Look, here they come."

Karina walks down the dock carrying a wicker basket. Violet is dressed in black with a cap pulled over her brown hair. The wind tugs at Karina's ball cap. She hands the basket to Violet and turns her cap around, pulling it snug over her short pink hair. They lug the basket down the dock, with synchronized footsteps.

I say, "I'll help them get onboard, and everyone will wear life jackets, no matter what."

Jacklyn grimaces. "We don't want a repeat of Jack's falling overboard."

"No, we don't. What a mess that was."

She says, "I know you were married to the man at one time, but he made some poor choices that caught up with him. But I wish Abby and Jack all the best."

I greet Violet and Karina, taking the basket from them and handing it to Jacklyn to stow inside. I offer my hand and help Karina and Violet step onboard.

In the cabin, they put on life vests, snapping the

plastic buckles shut. I say, "This may be a wild ride. The wind's picking up, and a storm's moving in. Are you ready?"

Jacklyn smiles, tugging on her yellow life vest. "I'm as ready as I'll ever be."

Violet and Karina glance at each other and nod. Karina says, "We're good."

Violet says with a slight smile, "Let's do this."

I release the dock lines, and we set off for whatever the future holds. Gripping the wheel, I steer away from an oncoming boat in the channel, and my stomach knots. I hope our adventure won't end in failure.

Gritting my teeth, I drive the boat into the bay, leaving the safe haven of the marina behind. Despite the risks and weather alerts warning of high winds, I'm backing Jacklyn's weird, wild rescue plan.

14

DUSTY

I swing by City Hall and spot my buddy Brad's car in the parking lot. He's in charge of the city planning department and oversees the building permit process. I pull over and park on the street and stride inside. I'll take him out for a beer and convince him to delay approving permits for my mother's project Stone Estates. I used to hang out at The Stag Tavern, where guys in construction gather after work, but lately when I walk in the door there, people grow silent and turn their backs on me. So, I'll offer to take Brad to the Brown Lantern instead.

I climb the stairs to the second-floor, march into the planning department and bang on a bell on the counter. Brad looks up from his desk in an office and comes out. We grew up together and when I owned Stone Construction, before my mom took it away from me, I was in here fairly often to check on permits for my projects.

He wears a half-smile and tugs at his collar. "Dusty."

"Hey, Brad. Can I take you out for a beer to celebrate the holidays?"

He glances around the empty office. "Can't leave. I gave everyone else the day off. It's just me today, holding down the fort."

"That's too bad." I lean against the counter. "I was hoping to talk to you in private about a personal matter."

His dark eyes dart around the room, and he shrugs. "Go ahead. You can talk here. What's going on?"

"You know the building site for Stone Estates?"

He shifts from side to side and crosses his arms. "Sure, what about it?"

I lean in and say in a low voice, "I heard there's an eagle's nest in a tree on the property."

His eyebrows jump up. "I hadn't heard that."

"It's against the Bald and Golden Eagle Protection Act to destroy their nests or eggs, so you might want to require an environmental survey before you issue final building permits. I'm just trying to keep you out of hot water. If the save the earth types heard about this, they'd raise a ruckus."

He nods and swallows. "Thanks, I appreciate it. Anything else you noticed, since you used to own the parcel?"

"Take a close look at the geotechnical report. The

prior owner dumped construction materials and fill, plus there's an underground spring. What looks like a wetland is adjacent to the building site, which would reduce the number of proposed homes. Drainage might be an issue too. You don't want sloughing and run off ruining streets and homes below. It might come back and bite you."

"Anything else?"

I scratch my chin. "Yeah, the site is barely within the boundaries to hook up to the city sewer line. Do you have enough capacity at the secondary wastewater treatment plant to handle additional sewage from these new homes or will you need to expand the facility? That'd cost a lot. The city might encounter hidden costs down the road."

"Got it." He jots down notes. "This is good stuff. Any other comments?"

I clear my throat and smile, skewering my mother's plans. I want her to crumble under pressure and give me back my company. "What about the water supply? Does the city have the capacity to serve a large new subdivision? Those will be big homes with three to four bathrooms each. Landscaping for pricey homes like that will probably suck up water in quantities we haven't seen before."

Brad writes something down and looks up, smiling. "Thanks, buddy, appreciate your help. You've got my back. And as the former owner, you know the property better than anyone else. No one has mentioned these concerns."

I shake his hand and grin. "Glad to be of help. I'm looking out for you, my friend."

15

JACKLYN

I cast off the dock lines and pull up fenders as Irena heads into Fidalgo Bay. A stiff wind blows from the north, blasting the boat with frigid air, and I go in the cabin, rubbing my hands together for warmth. Irena sits at the helm, humming a tune and steering through choppy whitecaps. Karina and Violet are quiet, and I mull over what we're about to do.

Rounding Heron Point, Irena turns west, entering Cedar Channel. The opposing current slows our progress, but Irena just chuckles, pushing down on the throttle. The boat picks up speed, and we plow through waves, sea spray flying up from the bow and over the sides.

I tap a toe and count the minutes until we arrive at the little dock on Cedar Island. I borrowed a boat there one dark night when I was running from Shore Lodge. If we get inside Shore Lodge today, it'll be my first time back since I escaped a few months ago.

Karina says, "It's a bit late to be asking this, but why aren't we signing in to visit your friends, like normal people, instead of sneaking in with a cover story?"

I clench my fists. "Because their families told the staff they aren't allowed visitors, that's why. Even my card was sent back. They're cut off from communication with friends and don't have cell phones or a way to get in touch with me."

Karina studies the floor. "Sounds pretty bleak."

I nod. "They're kept under lock and key with no contact with the outside world."

Violet says, "Will they recognize you? What if they've gone downhill since you left?"

I shrug my shoulders. "We'll see what shape they're in. The institutional environment would wear down even the most optimistic person."

"Not me," Irena says in a loud voice as she steers.

Violet says, "It'd be tough living there. Karina, promise me you won't put me in a place like that when I'm old?"

The boat rises up over a wave and thumps down in a trough. We hang on for dear life, and Karina says, "I'll take care of you when you're old, Violet. Don't worry. We're family. I wouldn't do that to you."

Violet says, "But if I have dementia and you can't care for me, I give you permission to put me in there. Just make sure they give me med's to make me happy."

Irena says from the helm, "Most people don't have the money to pay for a place as fancy as that anyway."

Cedar Island appears, and the two-story building looms ahead. My stomach sours at the sight of Shore Lodge, reminded of my son's betrayal. I say to Irena, "You didn't tell Dusty what we're doing, did you?"

"No," she says. "Of course I wouldn't."

I say, "I hope he won't figure it out. If he has a glimmer of our plans, he'll crash the party, and instead of ringing in the holidays celebrating freedom, we'll be turkeys."

Karina says, "No way that'll happen. Only someone insane would be out on a boat on a day like this."

"Hold on tight," Irena says. "Here we go."

I grip a handhold and she turns the wheel, heading for a dock on Cedar Island's south shore. Waves crash against the hull, the boat rocks back and forth, and sea spray flies up in the air. Normally, being at sea calms me, but not today.

I swallow hard. The engine whines, and the floor under my hiking boots vibrates.

Irena turns to us. "Almost there. Are you guys ready?"

My gut churns with acid, and I say, "Yes."

"You bet," Karina says in a tight voice.

Violet wears a grim expression on her face. "I'm ready to get off this boat."

I shake my head. "I picked a doozy of a day to do this. It's nasty out."

Violet says, "But if we waited for perfect weather, nothing would get done."

"Okay, listen up," Irena says. "The dock's full, so I'll raft up to another boat. Jacklyn, it might be the Boston Whaler that helped you escape before. Get on the other boat and run to Shore Lodge. I'll be waiting with the engine running for a fast getaway."

Approaching the dock, Irena says, "Jacklyn, drop the fenders, will you?"

I head out into the wind and rain and drop the plastic fenders down to protect the sides of the boat. The boat rocks, but I hold the hand rails with a death grip. Wind whistles past, and I say, "The storm won't stop us. We'll get home safe and sound."

I make my way to the cabin and stick my head in, saying to Irena, "When you come alongside, want me to tie up to the other boat?"

"Yes, and hold on tight." She slows our speed and turns the wheel, coming alongside a Boston Whaler. I tie off to a cleat on the other boat, fingers flying, and Irena comes out. She says. "It's a go for you guys. Don't take too long and good luck."

I take off my life vest, toss it in the boat and say to Karina and Violet, "Let's go."

We step on the Boston Whaler and jump down on the dock. My pulse races as we set off at a trot, feet pounding on the wooden planks, not knowing what lies ahead. I hope my disguise and our cover story will fly, so we'll get inside without a fuss.

I shudder at the sight of the two-story building as we hurry ahead. Please, I say to the universe, let us return to town intact with at least one Shore Lodge resident tagging along, freed from the confines of those stark walls.

16

DUSTY

I leave City Hall and drive, rounding a corner and calling an engineer who drew up plans for Stone Estates. Another driver honks and points at my phone, but I shrug. I know it's illegal to talk on my phone while I'm driving, but I don't care. Rules apply to regular people, and I'm above all that.

When the engineer answers, I say, "Hey, Gibson, Merry Christmas. I have a favor to ask you."

"Merry Christmas. What's the favor? Make it quick, because we're about to eat an early dinner."

"You know those plans you drew up for Stone Estates?"

"Yeah?"

"Is there any way you can change them and insert a mistake, like move the utilities, so they conflict with where the buildings will go?"

He's quiet for a moment and says, "It wouldn't be right. I can't do that."

"Listen, I'll explain it another time, but this'll help me out. They're my plans, and I paid for them."

"What's in it for me?"

"A lot of cash, especially if you do it right away."

"I don't know. It sounds sketchy. I have to stand behind my work."

I say, "My mom's in over her head. She's never worked in construction. If she steps down, she'll hand the project over to me, and I'll be the owner and foreman again."

"Doesn't she already have the plans and blueprints?"

"I'll sneak in her house and swap them out."

"I don't know. Let me think on it. I've got to go. The family's waiting."

I clear my throat. "Do it for me, and you'll be glad you did. Thanks, buddy. Have a Merry Christmas."

He hangs up, and I park in front of the house where I grew up. A man with a long gray beard walks over to the window and looks out. Who the heck is that strange guy?

I scowl and climb out, ready to confront the stranger. Rain drops hit my ball cap and bounce off the pavement. Going up a paved front path to the yellow bungalow, I notice the flower beds and lawn have been raked. Mom's back with all her energy and not down in the dumps like after Dad died.

I knock on the door and frown as a memory flies by. When I was a kid, my parents worked at their garden store and blabbed about plants at home. But building houses is much more interesting. While they slaved away selling delicate things that could shrivel and die in a storm, I'm creating long-lasting value. I pound on the door. "It's Dusty. Let me in."

17

———

MERCURY

Buddy barks and runs around, so I take off my headphones, cringing at the sound of someone thumping on the front door. I get up from a recliner and look out the front window. Jacklyn's son is pounding on it. No wonder she's keeping him at a distance, because only a jerk would act this way.

I swing open the front door and look up at a tall broad-shouldered man with a lantern jaw. His huge hands are calloused. I say, "There's no need to pound on the door. It takes me a while to get moving, and I had head-phones on."

Buddy races outside, chasing a squirrel across the yard.

Dusty pushes past and stomps into the living room, looking around. His big boots with a waffle sole leave a trail of caked dirt on Jacklyn's new carpet, which she likes to keep spotless.

I put my hands on my hips and say, "You must be Dusty, and your mom doesn't want people wearing shoes in her house. So, please take off your boots and leave them on the porch."

He strides into the kitchen and hurries down the hall to the bedrooms, opening each door. I wait by the open front door and catch a glimpse of Buddy barking at the base of a tree. Jacklyn's son sets my teeth on edge. The air around him almost vibrates with tension. If he was a violin string strung this tight, he'd snap.

He charges into the living room and crosses his arms. "What's the camp bed doing in my room? Who's staying here? And are you living with my mother? I don't even know who you are."

I swat away his suspicions with a hand, and he glowers. I'm no expert, but he strikes me as paranoid and narcissistic, a toxic stew. If I were mixing a cocktail version of him, I'd measure out an ounce of bitter ego, a dram of hot cayenne for seething anger, and a glass of lemon juice for his outlook on life. He must be insecure to act this way.

His cheeks are red, his hands are clenched, and he's breathing hard, with a bottled-up explosive temper that's barely suppressed, bubbling beneath the surface. I hope he won't lash out at me. I say, "You mom is testing out the camp bed for when we go camping this summer."

He comes close, towering over me. "Oh, yeah? What's all that food doing in the kitchen then?"

I wipe away spittle that flew out of his mouth, spraying my cheeks, and shrug. I'd like to get to know Jacklyn better, but if I offend her son or get into a fistfight with him, the future I envision is unlikely to unfold. Instead of hitting him in the gut, which is what I'd really like to do, I say, "She's getting a donation together for the food bank. That's what she said."

A vein throbs in his forehead. If he doesn't watch out, he's a candidate for a fatal heart attack, which killed his father. I don't mention it, because he's clearly already over the edge and ready to unleash whatever evil lurks inside.

"Who are you?" he says in a loud voice.

"I'm Mercury Thunder, and I've been seeing your mother the last few months."

He scowls. "Why didn't I know about this?"

I cock my head. "My guess is if you admit your mother against her will to a secure psychiatric ward when she's of sound mind, and you sell her garden store and are about to sell her home, that might push you apart. That might be why your mom isn't into talking to you, don't you think?"

His eyes blaze at me, but Buddy breaks the tension, trotting in with a dead bird in his mouth and dropping it at my feet like a prize. I'll have more to clean up before Jacklyn returns, with Dusty's dirt ground into the carpet and a dead sparrow before me.

Dusty leans down and looks me in the eyes. "Why aren't you afraid of me? You should be, old man. What's wrong with you?"

I fold my arms. "I've been through a lot. Not much surprises me anymore."

He stomps out the door. "Tell her I'll be back. We always eat Christmas Eve dinner together. I'm invited whether she likes it or not. It's a family tradition."

I say, "Did it ever occur to you that your family might be splintered and forever fractured, after what you did to her?"

He shakes his head and climbs in his truck, driving off in a cloud of exhaust. I cough and close the door. Shaking my head, I pat the dog and say, "You've got one messed up family, Buddy. Sorry about that."

18

VIOLET

I leave the warm cabin and follow Karina out to the boat deck, joining Irena and Jacklyn. It's raining, and the wind is picking up. Waves splash up in the gap between Irena's boat and the Boston Whaler.

I say, "I'll go first." I climb on the Boston Whaler, and Karina hands me a wicker basket. I take it in both hands, setting it down. I hold out a hand to Karina and then Jacklyn, helping them across. We grin at each other.

"Let's go," I say, moving over and stepping down on the dock. Jacklyn and Karina follow, and worn wooden boards tremble under our feet.

A rush of adrenaline floods my body, and I give Irena a quick wave before we set off down the dock. As rain peppers my face, I carry the basket, running toward land.

Ahead of us, a two-story hulking building is hunched behind a meadow. I swallow and review in my mind Jacklyn's drawings of the building's entry points and emergency exits. We dash across a two-lane road and turn, trotting up a lane toward our destination. Gravel crunches under my feet, and my armpits are damp with sweat. I snort at how Jacklyn believes the staff will show us to the secure second floor. But she's been here, and I haven't, so we'll try her way before improvising and gaining access through a service entrance.

Stay alert, Vi, I tell myself as we hurry ahead. Your job is to protect the others. Even though no one said it out loud, I know that's why they invited me along.

Jacklyn, who is strong and spry at sixty-one, reaches over and takes the basket from me. I say to her and Karina, "How're you two holding up?"

"Nervous as a goat on a hot tin roof," Jacklyn says.

I smile. I expected disaster, but this outing with untrained civilians is working out fine, so far. I'm here at Jacklyn's request to prevent her from getting locked in Shore Lodge a second time, which would be her version of a living nightmare, and to keep her out of jail, if possible. She's got the spark and sizzle I'd like to have at that age, so I agreed to assist on this mission and manage damage control if things turn bad.

Karina stops, holding her left side. "Got a cramp. Go on without me."

I pat her back. "Breathe into it. We'll wait. The lodge isn't going anywhere without us."

She furrows her brow. "I don't want to hold you guys back."

Jacklyn sets down the basket and puts her hands on her knees, breathing hard. "I was ready to stop. Good idea."

We're standing on the gravel driveway in the rain, as a car leaves the lodge parking lot with its headlights on heading our way. It's early afternoon, but we're losing light. Darkness is beginning to creep in. Huge storm clouds hover overhead, dropping cold hard rain.

"Hurry," I say, pointing to the forest. "Go in the trees and hide. We can't let them see us."

19

KARINA

I stumble off the road and hide behind a tall fir tree. Yesterday, I thought I was cut out for this outing with friends for a just cause, but in my heart, I'm just a scone maker, baker of quiche pies, and a potter and painter of canvasses. I'm not a hero, I'm just an ordinary person. I frown as a car drives slowly by and duck my head. I shouldn't have come along. I'm probably jeopardizing their chances of success.

Jacklyn comes over, stepping lightly through the forest, to stand by me behind the tree. She says, "How're you doing? Are you ready to go inside and work your magic?"

I blow out a breath and shake my head. "I'm sorry, I shouldn't have come. I'm not as fast at running as you and Violet, and I'm not as strong. I just stay indoors most days.

This is too much for me, and I'll mess it up, so you'd better go on without me."

Violet comes up and whispers in my ear, "You're brave, and you've made it through worse. Come on, sis, you can do this. We each bring a special skill, which is why Jacklyn picked us. Our team sticks together, and I have your back."

Feeling stronger, I nod and softly say, "Okay, I'll do it."

Jacklyn pats my arm. "When we go inside, I'll talk, and then you'll take over. Tell them how you baked this as a thank you for working with an underserved population. They're unsung heroes who deserve a huge thanks."

I wipe my nose with the back of my hand. "I can do that. Gigi always said to say something to make people feel better about themselves."

Violet says to Jacklyn, "Did you recognize the person driving that car?"

"Yes, it was Dr. Henderson, the head shrink and administrator. He didn't see me, so that's one obstacle out of the way. Hopefully, he isn't coming back."

Rains patters down through the tree branches, getting us wet. Water drips off my nose, and I wipe it away. I say, "I feel better now. Let's go."

Violet says in a stern voice, "Keep to the side of the road with your heads down, walking in single file."

We move down the driveway, gravel crunching underfoot, and approach the entrance to Shore Lodge. I will myself to slow my racing heart and blow out a long breath. The parking area is lit by floodlights, even though it must be two-thirty or three in the afternoon. I picture my grandmother Gigi smiling down at me, encouraging me to help others, and hope I inherited one iota of her inner strength. I don't want to disappoint my sister and Jacklyn by making a massive blunder, ruining their plan.

20

JACKLYN

I keep my head down as we approach the Shore Lodge parking lot. Butterflies flutter in my stomach, and I flinch when my phone dings. Violet tugs my arm and whispers, "Turn off your phone, or put it in airplane mode. We can't give away our position when we're roaming the halls inside."

"Sorry." I take out my phone and put it in airplane mode. Karina pulls out her device, touches it and tucks it in her pocket. I whisper, "I hope this is a new beginning for a few healthy unhappy residents."

Karina tugs on my puffer jacket. "What about the guy using the wheelchair? If he wants to leave, how will we get him to the boat?"

Violet says, "Don't worry about that. I'll handle it."

I take a deep breath and stride toward Shore Lodge, expecting the earth to open up and swallow me as I touch the cold door knob. I'm opening a door that will take me back into the building that housed my terrors. I was trapped as a child when a dirt tunnel collapsed on me, and ever since I've hated being confined in small spaces. Shore Lodge served up the terrifying feeling of claustrophobia on a number of unfortunate occasions.

I slip on a pair of pink over-sized glasses as a disguise and glide over to the reception desk with a grin plastered on my face. I might look insincere, but it won't matter. At least I'm giving off the essence of the holiday spirit. We'll catch them off guard and finagle our way into the secure second floor, where we'll convince them to let us out with residents in tow. I know it sounds like it won't work, but I've been dreaming of this day ever since I escaped. I've workshopped it in dreams and while walking my dog. There's more than a nugget of possibility that this odd plan will work out.

I place a hand on the reception desk counter, and the wood surface calms me at my core. We can pull this off.

The gal behind the desk looks up and smiles. Her generous mouth features bright red lips, and her cheeks are rosy. Her red and green sweater shows a Christmas tree.

I smile and say, "Hello, we're so glad to be here. My friends and I came all the way over from Millersville to sing carols for the residents on the second floor."

She tilts her head and peers at her screen. "That's wonderful, but I thought the carolers came through yesterday." She turns to a man with a ponytail in a white orderly uniform, who is sitting playing solitaire. "Didn't you think so?"

"Sure do. Heard they were pretty good too."

I pat the counter. "Well, I'm sure there must've been some sort of mix up, because we had it booked months ago. Our group is in so much demand, you know. It must've been a mistake."

She nods. "I suppose you could go up and entertain the residents anyway. Most of them won't remember what happened yesterday, and some might sing along. Music seems to calm them and brings back memories of happier times. I'll call upstairs to see if it's okay with the charge nurse."

I say, "Who's the charge nurse up there this afternoon? It wouldn't be Nurse Wright, that wonderful woman, by any chance? She has such a gift of gab, and she cares so much for her residents. Each and every one of them up there must feel loved and treasured by her."

Karina nudges me with an elbow. Violet crosses her arms, and I get the distinct impression they think I'm pouring too much syrup on the subject. Maybe I'd better back off a bit.

The receptionist checks her screen. "Nope, Nurse Wright isn't in today. We've got a new hire, and I'll give her a call right now." She talks on the phone for a minute and hangs up. "Okay, it's fine, and you're welcome to go up and sing. They'll send someone down to escort you to our secure second floor."

Putting my hands together, I smile and say, "Thank you. We're looking forward to entertaining shut ins who may appreciate a ray of sunshine on a dreary day. The waves out there when we crossed from Millersville just now were almost brutal. We're fortunate we got here in one piece."

The orderly stands and frowns. "I hope the ferry won't stop running due to high winds. I don't want to be trapped on the island overnight."

The receptionist waves away his fears. "People forecasting the weather get it wrong so often, let's not panic just yet."

Violet takes my hand and pulls me to the other side of the lobby before I talk my way into trouble by blathering too much. She gives me a fierce look, and I say in a loud, clear voice, "We'll share the joys of the season with others less fortunate."

Violet says in a low voice, "First step is complete. Step two, coming up."

I blow out a slow breath and fidget with my fingers. We've made it inside Shore Lodge and haven't been kicked out. Next, we'll enter the off-limits second floor.

Holding the basket, Karina leans toward me and says, "I'm taking the food upstairs, is that right?"

I exchange a quick look with Violet, and we nod to

each other. I whisper, "Wait until we're upstairs. Your scones are so good, they can open locked doors."

21

NURSE WRIGHT

Standing over the stove and stirring hot cider, Nurse Wright inhaled the aroma of apples, cinnamon, allspice and cloves. Her husband came in the kitchen, looked over her shoulder and said, "Guests will be arriving soon."

She smiled. "We're almost ready. Might as well enjoy ourselves." Her phone rang and she said, "I'll take this last call from work and turn off my phone. They should be able to handle it without me for two days."

He said, "I'll add the wine."

He poured a jug of red wine into the hot cider while she picked up her phone. It was the nurse covering the second floor at Shore Lodge, the new hire who was overwhelmed by what should be an easy job. Most of the residents were sedated and napped during the day. There was no need to panic, and Nurse Wright had trained the newbie for a month before leaving her alone on shift.

She answered and said, "Yes? What is it?"

The nurse said in a quavering voice, "I wanted to wish you a happy day off and tell you."

Nurse Wright snapped, "Tell me what?"

"Carolers are coming up to the floor to sing for the residents."

Nurse Wright shrugged. "I'm sure it's fine. Probably a scheduling mix-up, and we forgot to put it on the calendar."

"Okay. I just wanted to make sure before we let them in past the locked door."

Nurse Wright seethed inside but made her tone sound steady when she said, "This job is not the challenge you're making it out to be. You're in charge for two days, and it should be an easy, slow time over the holidays. I haven't taken two days off in a row in forever."

"Yes, I understand that. I just want to do the best job I can while you're gone."

Nurse Wright gripped the phone tight and resisted the urge to throw the device across the room. "Listen to me and hear me loud and clear. Do not call me again today or tomorrow unless the building is on fire. Understood? Only contact me if it is a real emergency."

"Understood. Have a good holiday."

"I'm trying to. Goodbye."

She hung up, turned off her phone and shoved it in

her purse. "I've had enough of babysitting my new hire. For the next two days, I'll ignore work and have a grand time. I deserve it after what I went through with that pain in the neck Jacklyn Stone."

Her husband grinned and poured a fifth of vodka into the mulled wine cider brew. "She was a thorn in your side. But now it's party time, here we go."

Her mother came out of the guest bedroom wearing a bright red Christmas sweater and red slippers. Her cheeks were rosy and her shoulder-length blonde hair was brushed. "Thanks for having me over to the island for the holiday. What smells so good?"

Nurse Wright's husband smiled. "It's our special Christmas drink. I'll get you a cup."

"Just a small taste," her mother said. "I don't want to fall flat on my face before the guests arrive."

Nurse Wright let out a contented sigh. All was right with her world and soon, friends would arrive, and they'd gather around the table telling stories into the night. This was the way to usher in Christmas, instead of working yet another shift at Shore Lodge. The alluring thought of retirement raised its appealing head, but she reminded herself she had ten long years left before she could sip beers on a beach in Mexico during the winter months. She said, "I'll make the mashed potatoes."

Her mother cocked her head. "Don't drop the bowl, like you did last year."

Hearing the word floor, Nurse Wright's mind swiveled

back to work, and she wondered how the new nurse would handle things while she was home with friends and family. She should have asked the barely capable young nurse if Florence had been taken to the infirmary. She scowled. And who were those unscheduled carolers, anyway? Was there a risk involved, with strangers entering the secure ward when she wasn't there overseeing and making sure all was going smoothly?

Her husband gave her a peck on her cheek, bringing her back to the present. He stood back and said, "I bet you're thinking about work, am I right?"

She took a mug of mulled wine from him. "You're right."

He sighed. "You promised to forget about work and enjoy the holiday."

She took a sip of the steaming hot beverage, inhaling the spicy aroma of the holiday spirit. "From this moment on, I'll be one-hundred-percent present for our party and won't give a fig about work. I'll kick back and enjoy myself."

Her mother giggled. "It's about time you cut loose, that's all I can say."

Her husband smiled and held up his mug. "It'll be our own holiday miracle, right here at home."

22

MARY

When my husband isn't looking, I slip into our study at home to print out more blank durable power of attorney forms, in case we need them. The printer hums, spitting out copies, and Fred walks by in the hall. He stops in his tracks, looking in, and I turn away, busying myself by loading paper in the printer tray. No need to get my husband who is an attorney involved.

He comes in and smiles. "What are you up to, dear?"

I shrug my shoulders and lean back, covering up a set of papers. "Nothing much."

He cocks his head, scrutinizing me, and comes closer. "You're usually in your art studio at this time of day." Glancing at the document behind me, he furrows his brow. "What are you doing?"

The printer stops, and I clear my throat. "It's for Jacklyn. No need to talk about it. Just something she's cooked up."

He folds his arms over his chest. "I see."

Seconds tick by. He eyes me, and I swallow, gazing back at him. This is why it's tough to be married to an attorney. He knows how to win arguments, like right now, when he's waiting me out. He knows I can't stand silence for too long. I grit my teeth and close my mouth.

He walks to the window and parts the curtains, looking out on a rainy early afternoon. "Are you by any chance helping Jacklyn with a secret project? Because I hope not. Months ago, she mentioned she wanted to return to Shore Lodge to help others leave. I distinctly declared I'd have no part of it."

I clear my throat. "Just pretend you never saw this. Go in the living room and read a book. Walk on past and forget about it."

He leans back against the window sill. Trees sway in the wind, and a branch hits the roof with a thud before dropping down in the front yard. I hope Jacklyn and the others are safe in this windy weather on Irena's boat.

He says, "I'm culpable and could be blamed for having knowledge beforehand and not stopping her. We can't back Jacklyn's effort to bring out people admitted by their families. I don't want either of us to be involved if she carries out her misguided idea."

I say, "She's our friend. We've got to help."

"Helping her could get us in trouble, from a legal point of view."

I cross my arms. "She's been through so much, and I promised to help her. I've got to do this."

He picks up the stack of papers, tucking them under his arm. "I don't suppose if I take these, it'll stop you from printing more?"

I wince because we always get along. We live a quiet life in a small town, and neither of us makes waves, until now. "No, it won't."

He sets the papers down and tidies the stack. "Now that I know you're helping her, you might as well tell me, when will she go to Shore Lodge? After New Year's, or in February, when the ferry to Cedar Island is shut down for annual maintenance?" He scratches his chest, the way he does when he's thinking hard. "I suppose she could enlist Irena's help and use her boat, in that event?"

I purse my lips but don't reply. After thirty years of marriage, we know each other well. From the gleam in his eyes, I can tell he's putting the pieces together, so I say, "It's best if you don't know the timing. Besides, I thought you'd be working in the yard today."

He gestures outside. "I was going to, but look at the weather. This is a day to stay indoors and read until we go to dinner." He half-smiles. "Jacklyn is on her way to Shore Lodge right now, isn't she?"

I slowly nod. "Jacklyn will murder me in my sleep when she finds out I told you."

He says, "This is a tricky situation. I need to think about the right approach. I could call and alert the facility."

I shake a finger at him. "Remove that thought from your brilliant mind. If you give Shore Lodge a heads up, it'll destroy Jacklyn."

He taps a finger to his lips. "Maybe we can find a way to work this out."

23

KARINA

Shore Lodge's lobby is decorated with heavy timber furniture and Pacific Northwest artwork featuring landscape paintings and wood carvings of salmon. A large window overlooks a manicured lawn and, beyond that, an untamed meadow and the gray choppy water of Cedar Channel, where foaming white caps rush past. I bite my lip and hope Irena is okay back at the boat.

Jacklyn wears a pair of over-sized pink-framed glasses, and she frowns, perhaps recalling how her grown children tricked her into coming here when she was grieving their dad's death. Our guide waves and walks over to us, looking fresh out of high school with stringy brown hair pulled back in a ponytail. She's wearing a white top, white pants and white sneakers. "Hi, my name is Darla, and I need you to sign in before I take you upstairs."

Violet and I sign in, listing our names and the time, but Jacklyn holds the pen in the air and says, "I normally don't put up with this kind of malarkey, signing my name so anyone can see it, but I'll do it today. We do so love to sing and entertain people."

She writes a name and signs on the printed form, and I lean over to check what she wrote. I put a hand over my mouth to stifle a giggle when I see she signed in as Woodruff Woodpecker. I hope we don't get caught because of her joke. I whisper to her, "Quite the risk."

She says in a quiet voice, "Don't be a worry wart. It's just a bit of fun."

I nod but suspect she's rebelling against the controls that kept her in place months ago when she was admitted to the psychiatric unit on the second floor. That would fan the flames of a deep-seated rebellion in any sensible, sane person. My grandmother wouldn't have put up with it, and I wouldn't want to be locked inside. But then it occurs to me that Jacklyn's name is known here, and she was smart to pretend to be someone else.

As we walk to the elevator, I lug the wicker basket. This place gives me the creeps and screams institutional setting. Part of it is due to the extreme silence, where you could hear a rolling pin drop on the carpeted floor. Everything is muted, with beige walls, tan industrial carpet, framed prints of bland woodland settings and blah coastal scenes. It's enough to put you to sleep. A little color on the walls wouldn't cause a riot to break out.

I get on the elevator and set the basket down as Jacklyn, Violet and our guide step in. The young aide reaches out with a bony index finger and punches a button for the second floor, and the elevator slowly rises. I swallow, and my ears click. I've never set foot in a psychiatric unit. I tell myself not to freak out, no matter what I see. I say, "What are most of the people on the second floor in for?"

Jacklyn nudges me and zips her lips in the time-worn signal to keep my mouth shut. She says, "You make it sound like a prison."

I shrug because I'm curious and say to the aide, "I just wondered, what's the most common diagnosis for residents in the secure ward?"

Jacklyn rolls her eyes, and Violet frowns, shaking her head ever so slightly.

The aide adjusts her ponytail and glances down at her shoes. "Our residents have a variety of conditions, including dementia. But I can't discuss it further, because it's private information protected by HIPAA. I'm sure you understand."

"I do. I appreciate your sharing that with me, and I'm glad we'll have a chance to sing for them. Maybe it'll brighten their day." I clamp my lips closed, because I'm nervous and carrying on. There's no need to go off the rails, as my grandmother Gigi would say, and keep talking too long. Let someone else have a chance.

The elevator doors slide open, revealing white walls

and a white linoleum floor. A splash of bold color would be a relief in this setting.

The aide says, "We ask that you keep a respectful distance from residents. Last week, a resident grabbed a visitor's wrist and squeezed hard, catching them off guard. Nurse Wright says for us to be vigilant, and prevention is the best policy for avoiding accidents."

I say to my sister, "Maybe they were lonely." Violet nods.

Jacklyn says in a tight voice, "How is Nurse Wright? I hope she's enjoying her holiday at home."

My jaw drops, and I stare at Jacklyn. How did she know a crucial nugget of information and not share it with us, her co-conspirators? From what Jacklyn told me in stories about her time at Shore Lodge, Nurse Wright is to be avoided at all costs, and I've been quaking in my boots, anticipating meeting her.

The aide eyes us, perhaps sensing tension between us and a crack in our trio's unity. "I'm not sure. You'll have to ask the charge nurse. How do you know Nurse Wright?"

Jacklyn brushes off with a wave of her hand, saying, "Oh, I've just heard in town how wonderful she is, that's all. Let's go over the concert line up again, gals." She turns to the aide. "We each have a favorite song we'd like to start with."

Brushing a stray hair from her face, the aide says, "I get it. I'm in a dance troupe in Millersville. It's normal to have creative differences and stage jitters."

The elevator comes to a stop, and I pick up the basket, holding the bottom. I can't wait to climb on Irena's boat and return to town. I say, "Absolutely."

24

———

DUSTY

I pull away from my mother's house and head for the marina. The old blowhard with the beard wasn't guarding Mom's house very well. I had time to search the rooms while he stood by the door. If I had found her checkbook, I would've ripped out a check, forged her signature and given myself a well-deserved Christmas gift.

I turn on the radio, tapping the steering wheel to the beat. Mom always serves Christmas Eve dinner at three o'clock, so she should be home cooking for her favorite holiday, with candles lit and strings of twinkling little white fairy lights hung inside the house. Something's off.

I park at the marina, hurry down the dock and stare at Irena's empty boat slip. She was evasive earlier at the fuel dock, and it's possible my mom is on Irena's boat. I'm bored, so I'll take my boat for a spin and see if I can figure out if they're together and where they went. Mom might be sniffing around Shore Lodge, because I remember her telling Aunt Mary she wanted to help people in the locked ward.

I roll my eyes. What a bunch of hot air. We're all only out for ourselves, so she might as well climb down from her high perch and stop pretending to help others and make the world a better place. She's not in touch with reality, unlike what her friends believe, and she was bitter when I admitted her to Shore Lodge, but I knew it was the right thing to do.

I stride down the dock to my boat and start the engine. The burgee on the bow flaps and flutters. Flipping on the marine radio, I listen for mention of Irena's boat. If I see her in the vicinity of Shore Lodge, I'll call Nurse Wright and let her know my mother may be in the area on a misguided mercy mission. If I had Mom's durable power of attorney over her finances and healthcare decisions, I'd put her back in Shore Lodge in an instant to keep her out of my hair on this side of Cedar Channel.

I shake my head. She didn't appreciate how good she had it, with a roof over her head and three meals a day at Shore Lodge. All she had to do was sit back, relax and enjoy the final ride to infinity, but she wouldn't accept her fate.

When the engine is warmed up, I release the dock lines and put the boat in gear, leaving the marina. I grimace, seeing a sailboat on shore on its side, reminding me to be careful in this storm. Since my mom took my company, I've been plotting ways to pay her back, like staging a home invasion to scare her. But even if I wore a mask and gloves, she'd know it's me from my height and build and voice, so that's out.

Driving the boat north to Cedar Island, I keep a lookout for Irena's boat. Waves crash over the bow, the boat rocks back and forth, and the brass bell clangs. I stand at the helm and tip back my head, laughing. If I can prove Mom is mentally unstable, I'll get my company back. Guys in the tavern will gather around, and I'll be the hero, buying rounds of drinks. I just need to drum up proof.

25

JACKLYN

I step out of the elevator, clenching my hands, and my heart beats fast, like a bird trapped in a cage. I follow the aide to a sliding glass door, the barrier that kept me from my dog and my home, and she taps her badge against a device. The glass door slides open to the surreal stark world of warehoused souls.

As I step into the secure unit, a shiver runs up my spine. If my son had his way, I'd live out my days behind this door, trapped in a glass cage without fresh air. I clear my throat and say to the aide, "Could we stop and see the staff before going in the dayroom to sing?"

She tilts her head. "Sure, but how did you know we were going to the dayroom? Have you been here before?"

I break out in a cold sweat. "Just a good guess is all. Karina here is a chef, and she brought baked goods for you all to share." Karina arches an eyebrow at me, because I stole her lines.

"Sure, I don't see why not." The aide leads us to the staff desk, where an orderly is tapping on a keyboard. Another aide in her fifties, I'd guess, is reading a book, but I can't see the cover. The book reader snaps her book shut when we approach, and she stands. The orderly looks up.

Karina holds up the wicker basket and says, "We're here to sing for your residents, and I brought homemade scones, quiche and coffee. Is there somewhere I can put this down?"

The orderly jumps up and extends his arms. "I'll take that. Let me help you."

The book lover says with a wide smile, "Thank you for thinking of us. Sometimes I feel like we're locked in and forgotten on this floor."

I shoot Karina and Violet a quick look and say, "I know how you feel. It's easy to feel lost and alone if you're not with family over the holidays."

We all nod, and Karina says, "I brewed strong coffee for you, if you like that."

The orderly tugs at his mustache. "Thanks, I was starting to feel sleepy."

Karina smiles. "Let's see what I brought." She pulls out a thermos of coffee and pours a cup, handing it to the orderly. Steam rises from the cup, making my mouth water. What I wouldn't give for a strong cup of coffee now, but it isn't a time to rest, it's time to connect with my friends here and make tracks for the boat. She says, "Do you take it black or with cream and sugar?"

He chuckles. "My last name is Black, and that's how I like my coffee."

"And how about you?" Karina says to the book lover. I sneak a peek at the book's cover and see it is a novel by Ken Kesey, inspired by his experiences working in a mental institution. How appropriate, if not unsettling.

The reader pushes up on her wire-rimmed glasses. "I don't drink coffee, just tea. But what smells so good? Did you mention scones?"

"And quiche?" says the aide who brought us up in the elevator.

Karina opens her arms. "We wanted to thank you for all you do here, working with a challenging patient population, and that's why we brought this for you." She unwraps the quiche, and the smell of cheesy-goodness wafts past. My stomach rumbles. Opening a container of scones, she passes them out, and the three workers dive in.

Our guide says with her mouth full and crumbs on her lips, "This scone is so good. Do you have a restaurant or something?"

Karina nods. "I own Gigi's Café in town."

The orderly's eyes open wide. "You're the owner? What happened to Gigi?"

Karina blinks back tears. "She passed away. It was unexpected."

Violet chimes in. "But she was getting on in years."

The book lover says, "It's never a good time to welcome death, even if you're in your golden years, like many of our residents. We call them residents, by the way, not patients, to give them the respect they deserve."

I shift my weight from side to side, growing impatient and wanting to get on with our task. Across the hall, a woman sitting in a chair screeches like a seagull swooping down to scoop up bread crumbs. Her hands are restrained, and she says, "Owls in the forest know. Hoo hoo. They'll tell you I'm right. He wouldn't leave me!"

The book lover brushes off her hands and goes over, telling the woman, "That's enough Mrs. Skidmore. Quiet down."

Mrs. Skidmore wails. "I want an ice bath."

"Not now. Maybe later."

Mrs. Skidmore catches my eye and hunches over, staring from a plastic chair in the hall. She jabs a gnarled finger in my direction. "I know her. She's back."

"Now, now," says the book lover.

My bowels curdle, and I rest a hand on my churning gut. If the staff on this floor knew I once lived here and escaped, they might tie me down too. I adjust my pink-framed over-sized glasses, turn away and unzip my jacket for something to do.

Mrs. Skidmore says in a hoarse voice, "Take me, take me with you."

I cringe, knowing she needs to stay put. There will be no rescuing Mrs. Skidmore today. From what I witnessed when I was here before, she requires full-time nursing care. She scratches her skin, leaving red welts, if she isn't restrained.

She says, "Take me to my husband and the witch he's with. They can't get away with what they did to me." She erupts in high-pitched jabbering and shrieks like a seagull.

A nurse wearing a white dress and sensible shoes strides out of the back room. She looks young, like she's just finished college. Her blue name tag with white letters says: 'Nurse Brown.' She says in a shaky voice, "What's going on? Keep it down, or you'll upset other residents. Nurse Wright says we can't have a rebellion on our hands."

Mrs. Skidmore hums before breaking into song. "I knew him when, the one who walked in the woods, the tallest of men among trees. And where did he go, the one who wandered, but down the street to Lorna. Oh, Lorna, Lorna in your pink fluffy slippers, what have you done to my husband?"

I wipe a tear from my eye. The orderly says to the nurse, "She's more lucid today. Must be the change in her med's, don't you think?"

The nurse nods and pulls out her phone. "I'll let Nurse Wright know about this change in behavior. She might want to come in and see it for herself. She doesn't want me to call her, but I guess I can text her to tell her what's happening."

My chest grows tight. If Nurse Wright comes through those doors, she'll haunt my life again. Nurse Brown frowns, staring at her phone. "Oh, no, she silenced her notifications. She never does that, but I guess she's entitled to a day off."

"Or two," the book lover comments.

Nurse Brown nods. "That's right, she has today and tomorrow off. I hope nothing bad happens while I'm in charge." She turns to me and says, "Hello, who are you? Are you the carolers they called about from the front desk?"

I plaster a fake smile across my face and gesture to Violet and Karina, who are beaming with generosity and rosy cheeks, looking like innocent cherubs with their hands behind their backs. "We're the Triplet Starlet Singers, and we're here to thank you for helping those who can't live on their own and sing songs for residents in a short concert."

Nurse Brown glances at a large round wall clock and turns her attention to me. "That's kind of you, and your red leggings are festive and fitting with the holiday spirit. But you'd better get on with it, because we have shift change coming up soon."

The young aide points down the hall. "The dayroom is this way. Come with me."

We follow her, and I sniff the air, smelling lemon-scented cleaning agents masking an odor of urine. To quell my nervousness, I blurt out, "You have two workers named Black and Brown. Isn't that a drink? No, that's a black and tan, that's right."

Violet and Karina elbow me, and the aide stops in her tracks outside the dayroom. She says in a low voice, "You might hear and see some disturbing sights while you're here, but know that our residents are well cared for."

I resist the urge to roll my eyes, recalling Nurse Wright's iron-fisted attitude toward me when I was living here due to my son's devious decision. But, I admit, some people require a place like this for nursing care and watchful oversight. It's just that I wasn't in that category. Instead, I was a grieving widow who had trouble remembering my name one time at the doctor's office. But Dusty dove on that like it was a loose football. He was delighted to pounce on my vulnerabilities and run off with my money.

We pause at the entrance to the dayroom, and I see two of my friends sitting side by side on the sofa. The angry man who was admitted against his will by his son isn't here and neither is Florence. I say, "I heard a woman name Florence lived here. Is she around? And an older man who used a wheelchair? I think his name was Jack?"

The aide meets my gaze. "You certainly are informed, aren't you? Are you sure you haven't been here before?"

I shake my head and cross my fingers behind my back. "Absolutely not. But we had hoped to sing for Florence and Jack. We have mutual friends in common. Isn't that right, gals?"

Karina and Violet nod their heads, bobbing like bobbleheads. "Definitely," Violet says. "Yes, you bet," Karina chimes in.

The aide leans in and says, "I probably shouldn't tell you this, but Jack left us, and Florence is in the infirmary. She was taken ill with a stomach bug."

My throat tightens with tears at the thought of Jack passing away. He was so angry at his son for forcing him to move here. I wince, because Florence being in the infirmary in the basement will make our job that much more difficult. "I hope the end was peaceful for Jack?"

She whispers, "He passed away in his sleep."

I pat my chest. "I'm sorry to hear that. We were hoping to meet him."

Karina and Violet nod, and Violet says, "Let's get started singing holiday tunes."

Karina links arms with her sister. "We love to sing."

The aide gestures to the front of the room. "Please introduce yourselves. The activity staff took the day off, otherwise we would've asked them to take you around."

I say, "No time like the present. Here we go, gals."

Stepping to the front of the room, we line up and link arms. I smile at my friends who live here, sitting holding hands on the couch. Billie and her wife wink at me.

I say, "Hello and Merry Christmas Eve. We're the Triplet Starlet Singers, and we're going to give you a short concert to celebrate the holidays. I'm Merry."

Karina says, "I'm Karina."

"And I'm Violet, her secret sister."

I hum the first bar and we break into an enthusiastic rendition of Jingle Bells. My two friends on the sofa smile, heads moving from side to side, and they join in, but other residents in the room doze in easy chairs, mouths hanging open.

Karina, Violet and I wrap our arms around each other's waists and sing Silent Night. In that crazy moment, I almost break down in tears, feeling supported in my wild endeavor and surrounded by loving friends.

I open my arms and smile at my two friends on the couch. "And now we'll sing a special rendition of The Twelve Days of Christmas. We made up this version, so you won't hear anywhere else."

I grin at Violet and Karina, and we launch into the song about twelve otters playing, eleven seals swimming, ten boats a-floating, nine seagulls swooping, eight eagles nesting, seven owls hooting, six coyotes yipping, five rowers rowing, four kayakers paddling, three deer eating, two crows cawing and one rescue dog running. By the time we reach the end of the song, my armpits are damp, and I'm swinging my arms for all I'm worth.

The aide steps away from her post where she's been leaning against the doorway and watching, and I whisper to Violet, "Take over and keep singing. I'll offer my friends a way out."

She smiles. "Go for it. We'll back you up big time."

26

JACKLYN

Karina and Violet sing about a snowman, and I slink over and perch on the couch by Billy, taking her warm hand in mine. I say, "Hello, my friend."

She smiles. "We're certainly surprised to see you."

The two women are dressed alike in cardigans with long braided gray hair, but they're quite different. Billy has a twinkle in her brown eyes, a hint of a smile and a lively, mischievous vibe. Grit is a wiry woman whose jaw is set.

Grit leans over and whispers, "You shouldn't have come back. It's too risky. They might admit you again."

I glance at their floral-patterned tops under sweaters and yoga pants with flip flops. They're not dressed for winter weather, and their footwear will be near impossible to run in.

My pulse races. "We came to take you out of here." I

pull out two forms. "Sign these, and we'll get them notarized in Millersville, so your families can't readmit you."

"Oh my." She turns and whispers to Grit, and they shake their heads. Billy says to me, "It's kind of you to offer, but we aren't going anywhere."

Grit adds, "We've made peace with living here."

My eyebrows shoot up. I hold out the forms, but they don't take them. I say, "If you want to leave with me, it has to be today."

Billy pats my hand. "You're a dear to come here, but we'd have nowhere to live."

My jaw drops. "We'll help you find a place to live. You'll stay with me at first. You can revoke your durable power of attorney and make a new one, like I did, to free yourselves from what your families did by locking you in here."

Billy shrugs. "Like we said, we're staying. It's not so bad. Meals are cooked and served. Bed linens changed. We're on easy street, unless Nurse Wright's in a bad mood and then we keep to ourselves. Duck and cover on those days, as you know."

I release a breath and say in a soft voice, "I guess I can see your point, and I understand."

She tilts her head. "We're not like you. We're get along gals, not rebels intent on burning down a building."

I say, "For the record, it was a small fire set back from the building as a distraction. I could've made it bigger, but I didn't want to hurt anyone."

Karina and Violet sing about a jolly Christmas, arm in arm. Karina gives me a look and raises her eyebrows, as if saying we'd better get going. Violet nods.

Billy says, "Did you get your garden store back?"

"No, but I did get my dog from the shelter and my house before it sold."

Grit wipes tears from her eyes. "It was the dog I was most worried about."

"Me too. That's what triggered my exit. I had to rescue him."

Billy squeezes my shoulder, giving me a side hug. "Stay strong, my friend, and fight the battles for us out there. We're quiet mice content in our quarters. Florence might want to go with you, but they took her to the infirmary. Don't know how you'll gain access down there."

I tuck the papers in my pocket and stand. "I've got a plan, and I hope it'll work. See you later, my loves."

I join Karina and Violet in the front, and we launch into an enthusiastic rendition of Rudolph the Red-nosed Reindeer. When the song ends, I say, "Thank you for listening, and we wish you a merry Christmas and a happy new year."

I throw a kiss to my two friends in the front row, who are clapping, and we wave goodbye, striding out of the room past residents dozing in vinyl easy chairs. I pause in the doorway of the dayroom and whisper to Violet and Karina, "We have to go to the basement."

Karina opens her hands. "How will we do that?"

"I have an idea."

Violet says, "Wait, what about your friends on the couch? Are they going with us?"

I shake my head. "They're staying, but I know someone else who wanted to go. The trouble is, she's in the infirmary in the basement."

27

———

IRENA

Eighteen-knot winds roar by the boat, and two-foot white caps froth in Cedar Channel. I drum on the steering wheel, wanting to race back to Millersville before the storm gets worse. The engine thrums, and the boat deck vibrates under my feet. I cross my arms and scan the shoreline for my three friends, but they're nowhere in sight. It feels like they're taking a long time.

Something thuds against the hull and I grab the boat hook, hurrying out in the wind. I push a log away, and the current carries it east. The wind howls, and boats at the dock tug on their lines. I let out a sigh, wanting to be home with my daughter on this wild, windy day. I send Kelly a text with a heart emoji.

I pick up my binoculars, studying the grounds around Shore Lodge. From what I can see, my friends aren't running through a meadow or racing down the gravel drive with people in tow, but I can't see the entire surrounding area, with evergreen trees blocking my view. I swallow and recall when my mom was sick, needing constant care at the end. There's a reason institutions like Shore Lodge exist. Some people need a place like that to call home.

A loud rumbling echoes from the sky, and with a whoosh, two military surveillance jets swoop overhead. My pulse picks up, and I duck out of instinct. Kelly and I took our friend's dog Happy to an off-leash dog park on Whidbey Island, and the pilots were practicing touch and go exercises. We could see the pilot's face in one jet as he touched down.

I draw a deep breath to calm myself and glance at the brass wall clock. Where are they? Why is it taking so long?

An orange helicopter flies overhead, and I chew on a fingernail. Please, don't let one of my friends need to be airlifted for emergency medical treatment. I furrow my brow because they might have been hurt in a scuffle in Shore Lodge. My mind runs amok with terrible possibilities.

I pace the floor near the helm. Whatever happens, I hope they remember to stay out of the basement. Jacklyn told me how she suffered there, and no one should have to go through that.

A gust of wind smacks the boat, and lines on other boats strain, pulling like racehorses ready to run. My boat is rafted to the Boston Whaler, and fenders between the two boats squeal and groan. I glance toward the bay and stare at a trawler-style powerboat headed my way. Jacklyn's son has a boat like that, but it can't be, because only a fool would be out in this weather.

I squint to see better, and Dusty waves from the helm. My hands turn cold, despite the heater in my boat warming the cabin. I have no idea what he's doing here, but his arrival doesn't bode well for my team.

28

———

DUSTY

Steering through choppy seas and aiming for Irena's boat, I leave the helm to drop fenders down over the sides of my boat. Wind lashes my face, and sleet stings my cheeks. An orange Medevac helicopter drones overhead. Waves slam into the boat, spraying over the sides. I hold onto hand rails and make my way inside.

My boat narrows the gap, and I watch Irena, who oozed confidence at the fuel dock. Her face is pale, and her mouth is pinched. She crosses her arms and glances toward land with a worried look, apparently waiting for someone. It's entirely possible that my mother is at Shore Lodge, intent on evacuating people.

Irena comes out of the wheelhouse into the wind, standing on her boat deck with her feet apart. Waves surge by, and her boat bobs up and down, tugging on lines tied to a Boston Whaler at the dock. I pull ahead and swing the wheel over, tucking my boat next to hers.

She fends me off with a boat hook, but I manage to tie a line to her cleat. She unties my line, but I wrap it quickly around the cleat again. We can play this game all day, but she's boxed in by the dock, and I have the upper hand.

I say, "Where's my mother? Is she at Shore Lodge?"

We stand on our boats facing off, hands on our hips, and she says, "Get out of here, or I'll cut your line. You can't raft up to me."

I shrug. "Don't tell me what to do." I glance at Shore Lodge and glare at Irena. "Tell me what's going on. Where's my mother?"

She reaches inside her boat, bringing out a long knife. "None of your business."

"She's at Shore Lodge making trouble, isn't she? That's why you were secretive, and she's not home cooking Christmas Eve dinner."

Irena narrows her eyes and clenches the knife. "I'll tow you into the channel if I have to. I'm warning you, don't raft to my boat." She looks back to shore.

I rub my cheek and consider my options. "I'll stay here until Mom comes back."

Irena cocks her head. "I dropped some people off, and they walked to the store. There's nothing going on that concerns you."

I tip my head back and laugh. "Right, nothing suspicious going on. Who goes for a walk in weather like this? No one. You're lying."

I grab my phone to call Nurse Wright and warn her that my mom is probably near Shore Lodge, intent on sabotaging something. Nurse Wright and I exchanged phone calls when my mother escaped from Shore Lodge, so I have her cell number. But she doesn't answer, so I leave a message saying my mom might be near Shore Lodge doing something suspicious. I hang up, shoving my phone in my pocket.

Irena's right eye twitches, and she marches over, casting off from the Boston Whaler at the dock. Before I can react, she puts her boat in gear and drives away, taking my boat, bound at midships to hers. She heads east, going with the current in the churning channel frothing with two-foot seas.

I grip the handrails, wind whipping past my face. Gritting my teeth, I consider untying my line from her cleat while we're underway, but I could end up losing a finger. My line is snug around her cleat, and the motion of being underway has tightened the knot.

I run to my helm and look around, thinking about what to do. When I turn my wheel, her boat is more powerful than mine, and my movement didn't alter our course. We round a point and head south in Fidalgo Bay.

I put my engine in reverse, figuring if I slow my speed, I'll be able to loosen the line and pull it off her cleat. My engine whirs, grinding out a complaint, but her boat carries us ahead. We head south at twelve knots, riding the waves, pushed by the wind.

Sweat drips down into my eyes, and I wipe it away. There's only one way to end this, so I grab a knife and run out, slashing the line binding us. The boats drift apart, and I hurry toward my helm as a big wave rears up, crashes down on the deck and covers me with frigid salt water. I shriek into the moaning wind and hold on for my life in the choppy sea.

Irena turns north toward Cedar Island. I race to the helm, wipe my brow and turn the wheel to follow her, but the boat bucks and thrashes in the waves, fighting the current and running against the wind. A blast of wind bears down, making the boat shudder. Waves rear up over the bow and smack down, throwing salt water up on the windshield.

I steer through the choppy mess, and a brass bell clangs with a warning that I should be in my marina slip, taking shelter, as any wise boater would do in these conditions. Gritting my teeth, I plot my revenge for being bested and place another call to Nurse Wright to warn her about my mother's possible plans. When she doesn't pick up, I shove my phone in my pocket.

The boat suddenly stops, as if held back by a hidden hand. I scowl and watch my speed drop to one knot. The line I just cut must be wrapped around my propeller.

My pulse races, and I scream into the briny wind. Stuck without power in the middle of a winter storm, my boat is drifting closer and closer to shore.

29

JACKLYN

Standing in the hall, I whisper to Karina and Violet, "I know we agreed to come to this floor, take my friends if they wanted to go and get out as fast as possible, but we can't leave Florence behind. She said she wanted to leave."

Violet crosses her arms and frowns. I rub my temples, where a headache throbs. A fake Christmas tree sprayed with a cloying scent reeks like toilet bowl cleanser. What a shame to do that to an innocent tree, even if it isn't real.

Violet checks her phone for the time. "It's past our rendezvous time at the boat. We've got to go meet Irena before we're caught."

The orderly clears his throat behind us, and I jump and let out a squeal. I hope he didn't overhear us talking. He wipes a crumb from his mouth. "I just wanted to thank you for the scones. They're delicious. Next time I'm in town, I'll stop by your café."

Karina beams. "Great, I look forward to seeing you there."

"And the quiche," he says, opening his arms wide. "It was so good."

Violet and Karina look at each other and smile.

He says, "I overheard you talking about catching a boat, but ferry runs for the rest of the day have been cancelled due to high winds and hazardous conditions."

I gulp. "A friend brought us over on her boat, so we should be fine."

He nods. "You might want to leave now, because they issued a small craft warning, due to gale force winds."

Karina bites her lip, gazing at me. Violet eyes me. I draw a deep breath and say, "Thanks for telling us, and you're right, we need to get going. Before we do, there's one last stop on our jolly caroling tour to brighten people's lives."

He tilts his head. "What's that? On the first floor?"

"I promised we'd stop in the infirmary to see one of your residents, Florence. Would you please show us the infirmary? We'll sing for Florence and when we get back to town, we'll tell people in Millersville about your amazing facility. Word will get around, and more people will want to live here. Won't that be wonderful?" I smile, knowing I buttered it on a bit thick, but I had to try my hardest.

He shrugs. "Sure, I'll show you the infirmary. Right this way."

We walk down the hall, and Mrs. Skidmore, restrained to a plastic chair in the hall, says in a shaking voice, "I know who you are. You belong here."

I gulp and shake my head, looking away.

The orderly says, "Hold on, and I'll get your basket. That was kind of you to think of the staff."

Violet frowns at me. Karina stares at a gray-haired resident shuffling down the hall with her pink cardigan on backwards. I hum a tune and tap a toe. We've got to go. We should be at the boat by now, where Irena will be waiting in worsening weather. But I can't walk out of Shore Lodge this time around without offering sanctuary to Florence. She dearly wanted to leave before, but I left her behind.

The orderly hands Karina her basket and thermos, and we set off for the elevator.

Behind us, Mrs. Skidmore calls in a trembling voice, "Jackie, take me with you."

I press my lips together and count the seconds until we're freed from this sterile airless floor, where I might be found out. The orderly presses a button for the elevator, and when it arrives, we step onboard. He taps his badge against a device on the wall and pushes the button for the basement. As the elevator descends, I let out a sigh of relief. The farther we are from the secure psychiatric unit, where white institutional walls close in on me, the better.

He says, "It's unusual for Mrs. Skidmore to speak

clearly, like she did just now. Her speech is usually garbled and littered with phrases and bits of songs. Are any of you named Jackie? Do you know Mrs. Skidmore?"

My face blazes hot enough that we could use the energy to light Millersville at night. Nurse Wright called me by that name, but I disliked it. Maybe Mrs. Skidmore, despite her rantings and ravings, knows more than she lets on.

I shrug and recall my departed husband Albert saying, "Honest is the best policy." Except he didn't follow that in his own family life about money, or disclose his heart condition to me before he died. I say, "When I was a kid, people called me Jackie. But it's just a coincidence."

He scratches his chin. "Strange."

Violet makes a motion for me to zip my lips, and I nod. Karina raises her eyebrows. I swallow, and my ears click. I can't wait until we're running away and racing for freedom on Irena's boat.

The elevator doors slide open to the basement. Cool air carries the aroma of a submarine sandwich. The orderly guides us around a corner, and a young woman sets down her food and opens her arms, giving me a huge hug. I whisper in her ear, "Don't use my name."

Stepping back, I say, "How wonderful to see you. We've come to sing carols for Florence, if she's up for it."

The orderly glances at us. "Do you two know each other?"

I say, "Sally is my friend, and we met on a trail going up Cedar Mountain. The one with the cell towers on top."

He rubs his upper lip. "Sure, I've been on it. Sally, okay if I leave them with you? I've got to finish my shift and clock out. The ferry stopped running, if you haven't heard, so I need to find a place on the island to crash tonight."

She nods. "You go ahead. They'll sing a few songs, and I'll sign them out."

The orderly leaves, closing the door behind him, and she turns to me and frowns. "I offered to help, but I can't jeopardize my job. What're you doing down here?"

"We need to see Florence. I'd tell you more, but it'd get you in trouble."

She lets out a sigh. "Fine, but make it quick. Come on, I'll take you in there."

30

NURSE WRIGHT

Nurse Wright glanced at the dining table set with candles, red placemats and greenery cut from their property. A fire blazed in the fireplace, but outside, harsh wind battered the house, making window panes rattle. Her mother sat by the fire in an easy chair reading a mystery. "More mulled wine?" Nurse Wright asked.

Her mother shook her head and looked up over her reading glasses. "Not yet, or I'll fall asleep during dinner. How's the prime rib looking?"

Nurse Wright's husband said, "We cranked up the oven heat, put the prime rib in and turned off the oven, but we can't open the door to look or we'd let the heat out."

A gust of wind shook the house, and the lights flickered and went out. "I bet the power's out on the whole island," Nurse Wright said. "But at least they have a generator at work."

She picked up her phone, taking it off airplane mode, to call their guests and let them know about the power failure. As she was about to dial, she noticed a call had come in from Dusty Stone. But she don't have time to listen to his voicemail, so she ignored it.

Her mother said, "What's going on? You look confused."

"The son of the woman who escaped from Shore Lodge called, which is odd."

"He probably wanted to wish you happy holidays."

She nodded. "Could be. I'll call the Pearsons and tell them the power went out and to bring flashlights."

Her husband chuckled and said, "And blankets and snacks. Tell them to bring chocolate and plenty of it to go around."

Nurse Wright smiled. "Comforted by chocolate and the fine company of friends, we'll weather the storm."

As she dialed, an unpleasant thought crossed her mind, and she frowned. Dusty might have called about his mother making trouble at Shore Lodge. Nurse Wright was still digging out from the paperwork nightmare Jacklyn Stone caused. Jackie was trouble, through and through, and Nurse Wright never wanted to see her again.

31

JACKLYN

Sally stops outside a room and says, "Wait here while I ask Florence if she'd like to see you." My fingers curl into fists, knowing the clock is ticking, and we're on borrowed time. We've got to get back to the boat before we're caught.

A moment later, Sally opens the door wide and waves us into a small room, where Florence is resting in bed. Her face is pale under her red bird's nest of a messy wig.

Florence breaks into a smile. "I know this trouble-maker." I step forward and open my arms to hug her, but she says, "I've got a bug. Don't get too close."

I shoot Karina and Violet a worried glance and ask Sally, "Is she contagious?"

Sally shakes her head and says to Florence, "You're fine now. I'll send you up to the second floor in an hour or so."

I grimace and say. "Where the air around Nurse Wright will make you sick."

Sally pats my shoulder. We met when I lived here a short time, and she was kind to me when my world was falling apart. After I made it home to Millersville, we stayed in touch.

Sally says, "Let's not forget, for some people, it's the best place for them to live."

Florence screws up her face. "My family stuck me in here."

I turn to Sally. "Would you please give us a moment? It'll just take a few minutes, but I have something to say to Florence. Thanks."

Sally puts her hands on her hips. "You should sing, in case someone comes down here and asks what you're doing."

I nod. "Ready, gals?" We launch into Silent Night and switch to Jingle Bells in an upbeat medley. I close the door while belting out lyrics, and we stop singing. I say, "Florence, we can take you to Millersville right now, if you want to leave for good."

Her eyebrows shoot up. "My family won't agree to that. If I try and they catch me, Nurse Wright will make my life miserable. When you left, she took it out on the rest of us, marching around in a bad mood. I can't risk it, and I don't want my family to be angry with me."

Karina says, "I'm Karina. Were you admitted against your will?"

Florence nods. "That's right."

Violet says, "We could take you to Jacklyn's place and, after that, we'll help you figure out where to live."

Tears well up in Florence's eyes. "I've always wanted someone to show up and take me away from this place, and I admire you, Jacklyn, for having the courage I lack. But I'm too chicken to leave and face my family's wrath. I don't want to find a new place to live or make a change at my age, so I'll pass. But thank you, and just recalling this moment will help me get through the months ahead."

My jaw drops. "You said you wanted to leave, but now you don't want to?"

She cocks her head. "I was grumbling for the sake of complaining, so don't mind my nattering negativity."

I pull out a form and say, "If you want to leave, sign this to revoke your durable power of attorney. You can live a new life."

Violet says, "But we've got to leave right now and run for the boat."

Florence says, "I'm too weak to run. I'm not strong, like you are Jacklyn. Besides, I get seasick on boats, and I'm deathly afraid of them. So, no thanks, go on without me."

I pat her shoulder. "Are you absolutely, positively sure?"

Violet taps a toe. Karina bites her lower lip. You could cut the tension in the small room with a pair of pruning shears. I stuff the papers in my pocket and pat Florence's shoulder.

She sighs. "I appreciate your kind offer, and I'll never forget this, but I've made peace with my situation. I don't want to find a new place to live. This is the last stop for me."

I say, "I understand and know that I'll be thinking about you."

Florence dabs her eyes with a tissue. "Goodbye, my friend."

My hands tremble, and my heart races. At any moment, we could be caught. I say, "I'll be sending you love."

Karina sets down the basket. "This'll slow us down on the way to the boat, so I'll leave it."

Violet says to me, "We've got to go. Will you distract Sally, and we'll slip out?"

"We'll take the stairs to the first floor and run for our lives before they trap me in this infernal place again."

"Bye, Sally," I say, striding past her to the stairwell. "Sign us out, will you? We're the Stardust Triplet Singers."

"Will do," she says with a crooked smile. "Get out of here before they catch you."

Climbing the stairs, I say, "Sashay through the lobby like it's no big deal until we're outside. Then we'll take off for the boat."

"Got it," Violet says.

Karina says, "I thought we were the Starlight Triplets. Not Stardust."

We come out into the lobby, breathing hard. Hurrying

along, we look straight ahead. I don't want to jinx our departure by catching a watchful staffer's attention. Violet says, "I like the name Starlight Singers, and I thought we sounded pretty good."

Karina grins. "Or The Secret Starlight Singers. We could sing in my café."

We approach the front door and step over the threshold. The door closes behind us with a click, and we run down the gravel drive to the boat, our feet flying at top speed for freedom.

Crossing a two-lane shoreline road, we stumble down a dirt path to the dock, panting and out of breath. But when we come to the Boston Whaler, we stop and stare. Irena's boat is nowhere in sight.

32

IRENA

Leaving Cedar Island behind, I tow Dusty and his boat away from the dock where Jacklyn is due to appear at any minute. A strong current carries us east, and the wind howls, as a winter storm bears down from the north. I glance over at Dusty, scowling at his helm, and I say, "Bet you didn't expect me to haul you away from Cedar Island. Don't mess with me or your mother."

Past Heron Point, I head south in Fidalgo Bay. Waves crash over the bow, and the wiper blades squeak. We're going with the wind and current, riding what are now three-foot waves. I'll drop him off and race back at top speed to pick up the crew, and because his boat is slower, he won't be able to catch up or stop us.

I could drop him near the tide flats. My boat's draft is

three feet, and his is six, so I'll skim over shallow areas, while his hull will run aground. But I let out a sigh and shake my head. That's something Dusty would do, but I won't mimic him. I'll rise above dirty fighting and take him away from the action. If anyone deserves bad things to happen to them, it's Dusty, for how he treated his grieving mother.

A seagull flies past, flapping hard and fighting the wind. Dusty is a whack-a-mole man, popping up despite people in town shunning him. He keeps coming back to bother Jacklyn, even though she's been clear about not seeing him. She told him not to come back unless he's invited, but he hasn't paid attention to her requests. He's tone-deaf in the orchestra of life.

Dusty comes out from his wheelhouse holding a long knife. My shoulders tense, and I slow our speed, grabbing the boat hook as a weapon. He reaches out and slices the line binding our boats together.

His boat slips behind in the distance, and I turn the wheel, heading north for Cedar Island. "See you later, nasty pants. Good luck keeping up with my boat. You'll never catch up."

I push down on the throttle and bring my speed up to fifteen knots, plowing through whitecaps and inhaling briny sea air. My thoughts return to my teenage daughter, who is alone at home. When I was Kelly's age, I spent Christmas Eve and Christmas by myself in our apartment while my mother worked.

A lump forms in my throat, and I drive the boat toward Cedar Island. I've got to get home, because nothing matters more than my daughter.

33

DUSTY

I slam a fist on the dashboard, bellowing with rage. I've lost power and am moving dangerously close to shore. I need a tow to the marina, and a diver to go down in frigid water to cut a line off my propeller. I snarl, "What more could happen? I deserve better."

I rub my cheek and frown because the only person I know to give me a tow in the storm is Irena, and she foiled my plans to thwart my mother. Waves slam into the boat, and I grab a handhold. I've got to call for help over the marine radio, or risk running aground on the tide flats.

I grind my molars. Everything was easy before my dad passed away. He gave me money for my construction company when I asked, and I didn't have money worries, not until my mother took a close look at her finances.

Sniffing the air, I smell salt air and scowl. I shouldn't be out in a storm. I should be at my mother's house eating turkey dinner with cranberry sauce and all the fixings. It's her fault that I'm out here, and I'll think of ways to get back at her. But first, I must save my boat and my life.

I pick up the microphone for the marine radio, hold down the button and say, "Mayday, mayday, mayday, this is a thirty-four-foot powerboat in Fidalgo Bay. I lost power and am about to run aground."

The Coast Guard comes on. "How many people are on board?"

"One, it's just me. The wind and current are pushing the boat toward shore."

"How close are you to shore?"

My throat is dry. I swallow and say, "Forty yards and getting closer with each minute."

34

JACKLYN

I bend over with my hands on my knees, panting and staring at the gray choppy water where Irena's boat should be. The Boston Whaler, blissfully unaware of our plight, bobs at the dock. I was wrong to drag my friends out in a storm. This whole venture was a waste of time and trouble. Wind whooshes past, and trees onshore sway back and forth. I pull down my hat over my ears and swallow tears of shame.

Shoving my hands in my pockets, I say in a tight voice, "Irena promised to wait for us. Where is she?"

Violet and Karina won't meet my gaze. They stare at white-caps rushing past.

I crane my neck, searching for Irena's boat, but see no sign of her. Goosebumps prick my flesh under my festive holiday red leggings, and a dark feeling of doom washes over me. I clear my throat and say, "I'm sorry I dragged you into this. It's my fault we're stranded and have no way off the island."

Violet tugs on her black watch cap and scans the channel. "Let's not panic. I'm sure she's on her way. We'll figure out a way to get home."

Karina says, "It's not like we can call an Uber."

The temperature drops, and I stomp my cold feet. Sleet stings my cheeks. Wind whistles through boat masts and halyards clang, but I'm not in the mood for a mariner's concert. I want to go home, see the best dog in the world and have dinner with Mercury, my new friend.

I pull out my phone and call Irena, but she doesn't pick up. My throat grows tight with tears, and I wince. I'm no hero, I'm just a nobody who owned a garden store. Why did I think I could correct a bad situation for a few Shore Lodge residents? It's clear I was a fool, because no one wanted to go with us, except Mrs. Skidmore, who is smarter than she appears at first glance, but sadly there will be no starting over for her. I blow out a breath and stare at a rotten plank in the dock, where a raised nail head sticks up. My so-called rescue mission turned into a flopping fiasco.

Fierce wind blows past, howling and moaning. I blink back tears and say, "I had no business dragging you out in this storm. We didn't get justice for four people admitted against their will, and you could've stayed home, but no, I dragged you out on a fool's errand. But I appreciate what you did today. Thank you so much."

Karina exchanges a look with her sister and says, "It was worth it, because you gave them a chance to start over. They're probably smiling and feeling better, just because they had a choice. I know if I were stuck in that situation, I'd want someone to offer me a way out."

Violet nods. "That's right. We gave them the choice, and I'm glad we did. Plus, it was interesting to see a psych unit up close for the first time." She shudders. "That woman in restraints, Mrs. Skidmore? She almost got us caught. That was a close call."

An older man jogs down a dirt path to the dock. "Wait," he calls, "wait for me."

Wood planks tremble under my feet as he runs, and his ears stick out from under a brown knit cap. I recognize him from my time on the first floor at Shore Lodge, when we were in a support group together. He talked about playing the trumpet and told stories about being in a circus band.

He stops in front of us, panting and looking over his shoulder. "I've got to get off the island before they catch me. If you're waiting for a boat, can I go with you?"

I say, "Our friend should be pulling up in her boat any minute, we hope."

He stomps his feet and rubs his hands together. "Any minute isn't soon enough. They'll come for me and bring me back."

My pulse picks up, recalling when I ran away from Shore Lodge, and I say, "Don't worry, we'll help you."

He flicks his gaze to the road. "Thanks."

Snowflakes fly past, and he shoves his hands in his pockets. "I heard you got away, so I'm not sure why you'd come back. Do you still own a garden store?"

I glance toward the road and hope Nurse Wright and Dr. Henderson with his trimmed goatee won't appear and drag this poor man back to their facility. I shake my head and say, "My son sold it when I was admitted to the second floor. I learned I can't trust my relatives, but I can count on my friends, like these two. This is Violet and Karina. They're sisters and live in Millersville."

He tugs on an ear lobe and glances at the road. "Nice to meet you. I'm Del, and I know what you mean about trusting relatives. I'm worried Shore Lodge will send someone to haul me back inside, but I couldn't take it anymore. I want my old life back, with some modifications."

I cringe, picturing Nurse Wright swooping down on her day off to capture him. "I get that. The ferry's down, so I hope our boat will get here soon."

He scratches his whiskered cheek. "Me too."

Karina points at a boat coming our way. "That might be her."

But a white-hulled power boat goes past, heading west toward Rosario Strait with sea spray flying up as the boat smacks into waves, bucking the current.

Del shifts from side to side, clenching his fists. My mouth drops open when two cars screech to a stop on the shoreline road, and Nurse Wright hops out of an SUV. She's joined by Dr. Henderson, the head of Shore Lodge, who exits a black sedan with tinted windows.

My pulse pounds in my ears, and I exchange a quick look with Violet and Karina. We glance around in a panic, but we're stuck on the end of a pier with no way out.

They run down a dirt path toward us, and Nurse Wright shouts, "Stop her. Jacklyn Stone, I'll have your head for helping him."

I say to Violet and Karina, "I'll look for a key to this boat and see if I can drive it." I climb on the Boston Whaler and search under cushions, near the helm and by the marine radio for a key, but come up dry as an August day. We can't let Del be hauled back to Shore Lodge, and I can't survive being admitted a second time, if they make up nonsense about my mental acuity. Nurse Wright would retaliate for my escaping if I were behind those walls again, and I'd lose the sanity I have left.

Nurse Wright yells, "Grab him."

My palms grow moist, and I yell, "I can't find the key, but climb on board, so we're ready for Irena."

Sleet stings my cheeks, and my pulse races as I help Karina, Violet and Del step onboard the Boston Whaler. We move to the other side, away from the dock, and the boat rocks. Wind whistles past, and boats at the dock tug on their lines. We all want to be set free today. I glance toward the channel, where Irena's boat is racing our way, and say, "Here she comes."

"Stop," Dr. Henderson says, a wild-eyed look on his face. His salt and pepper goatee is as trimmed and tidy as ever. For a moment, it's as if I never left Shore Lodge, with them closing in, waving their hands and frowning.

Nurse Wright calls, coming closer, "Don't let him get away. Grab Stone. She needs to be taught a lesson."

But Dr. Henderson trips and falls flat on his face, where the nail was sticking up. He groans. "I'm hurt. I can't get up. You've got to do it."

Irena brings her boat alongside the Boston Whaler, and I say, "Be careful." I help the others step across the choppy gray water onto her boat.

Nurse Wright says, "Stop right now. Come back here."

I'm about to jump over the frothing water between the boats, but I'm stopped by a hand grabbing me from behind, and I'm pulled toward the dock. I lunge away with all my strength, and my puffer jacket rips.

Nurse Wright screams, "Grab her. They're getting away."

I leap across the water onto Irena's boat and stick my head in the cabin, saying to Irena, "All onboard. Take off."

I hold on to a railing and crane my neck, looking back at the dock as Irena drives away. Doctor Henderson is getting up, shaking a fist, anger written all over his flushed face as we depart. Nurse Wright holds a ripped piece of fabric in her raised hand. Her face is red, and flecks of spit fly from her lips. Our eyes meet, and she shakes a fist, yelling something I can't make out.

Stepping inside the cabin, where a heater whines, blowing out hot air, I whoosh out a relieved breath and let my shoulders relax in the warmth.

Irena says, "Fasten your life vests and hold on tight."

I pull on my life vest and stare at the two-story building looming above a meadow on Cedar Island. "Good riddance, Shore Lodge. We got out and lived to tell about it."

Irena pushes on the throttle, and the boat surges ahead, plowing through three-foot waves. Salt water sprays up over the bow, covering the windshield. We're in for a bumpy ride. Irena turns at Heron Point, leaving Cedar Island behind and heading south toward the marina.

Del, the trumpet player from Shore Lodge, tenses his jaw, and his left eye twitches. He says in a shaky voice, "That was close."

Karina says, "But we made it."

Violet grins. "The outcome wasn't what we expected, but the mission was a success."

I smile. "I think so too. Welcome, Del."

He wipes his brow. "You bet."

I clear my throat. "If Dr. Henderson calls the police

and they meet us at the dock in Millersville, is there any reason they could cart you away to Shore Lodge?"

He scratches his chin. "They might concoct an excuse, but on paper, I voluntarily admitted myself, so I should technically be allowed to leave at any time."

"We'll see what happens when we get to the other side."

The marine radio erupts. "Mayday, Mayday, Mayday," a man says. "I've lost power and I'm drifting to shore. I'm in Fidalgo Bay."

I cock my head, because that sounded a lot like my son's voice.

The Coast Guard talks with the skipper before asking boaters in the vicinity to assist the vessel in distress. When no one answers, Irena reaches for the marine radio microphone and says to us, "I'd better take this."

She holds down the microphone button and says, "Nimbus Boat Rescue is in the area and can assist. What's the skipper's phone number and his position?"

I gulp when I hear my son's phone number and imagine his boat washed up on shore. When Irena hangs up, I say to her in a low voice, "Dusty issued the distress call."

Irena increases our speed. "We have to get there before he runs aground."

I blow out a breath. Dusty undermined me at every turn after my husband died, but he's still my son. I don't want him to die in the Salish Sea in a shipwreck. "Whatever I can do to help, let me know."

Del clears his throat, and his pale face has a sheen of sweat. We surge over a swell, and he says, "This is a rougher than I expected."

Irena floors it. "Not a day to be out boating unless you have to. Hold on."

Karina and Violet grip handholds. Their jaws are clenched, and they stare straight ahead as the boat bounces in choppy water, rocking from side to side. I hold onto a handhold and brace myself.

A wave crests and thumps down on the bow, covering the windshield and obscuring our vision. I curl my toes and hope we'll get to my son before his boat runs up on a rock.

Del says, "Is it always this rough?"

"Nope," Irena says in a calm, steady voice. "You never know what to expect, especially in winter. But Jacklyn insisted today was best to breach the walls of Shore Lodge, so off we went."

He says to me, "They're short staffed for the holidays. I saw you enter the building because your red leggings caught my attention. Did you manage to go up to the second floor?"

I say, "Yep, and down to the infirmary, but no one wanted to escape with us."

"Probably afraid to start over. I can understand that."

Karina says, "I can too. Starting over can be scary."

Del asks, "Are you going to the marina in Millersville?"

Irena nods. "Yep, after we make a stop to help Jacklyn's son."

He turns to me with wide eyes. "Your son made the distress call? The one who sold your store without your permission?"

I nod and hold on for dear life. "That's the one. But no one deserves to die at sea today, not even my no-good son who cares only for himself."

Irena moves her chin in the direction we're heading. "There's he is, just ahead."

South of us in Fidalgo Bay, a power boat thrashes in churning waves. Being aboard that boat would be a carnival ride. Maybe this experience will wash some sense into my son's head, and he'll come out of it thinking of others for a change, but I doubt it. He sold my garden store and was selling my home in a me, my, mine gesture. But the worst of it was how he put my dog Buddy in a shelter while I was locked away.

I frown at how Dusty sponged money off my husband and me for years to fund his construction company. But it's my fault I trusted the wrong person with my durable financial power of attorney. I opened the door to be taken advantage of and did it to myself.

His boat comes in closer view, and I frown because my money probably paid for his boat. That's the last time I'll trust the wrong person with my life. Never again.

A gust of wind batters the boat, and Irena grips the

wheel, fighting at the helm to stay the course. The boat plows into a three-foot swell and surges ahead, salt water spraying. It's nuts to be out in a storm, and it's all my fault.

Irena says, "Jacklyn, when we get close, drop the fenders. The rest of you, wait for my instructions. This'll be tough, but we'll get the job done."

I lick my dry lips and hope she's right.

35

DUSTY

I issue a distress call, slamming down the marine radio microphone. My stomach sours as the shoreline comes in clearer view, and I clench my fists, screaming in frustration. If not for my mother, I wouldn't have gone out in this rotten weather. I'll make my mother pay for this.

Waves jostle the boat, and the hull shudders and groans. I wipe beads of sweat from my brow. I've got to do something. I can't wait and drown.

I pull on a wool cap, jacket and work gloves, turn on the windlass and step outside, making my way through the wind to the bow. I look around the bay for boats to help me, but in this nasty weather, everyone sane is at home. I release the anchor, and it drops down into the churning water with a splash. Letting out the anchor chain, I hope it will slow my speed to shore.

My heart thuds in my chest, and I make my way to the helm, keeping a tight grip on handholds. But the boat thrashes in rough seas, bucking up and down and rocking violently from side to side. Waves splash over the sides, soaking me in frigid salt water. Before I return to the wheelhouse, I turn and scream into the wind. "Damn you, this is your fault!"

36

IRENA

I grit my teeth and steer through the storm. The wind opposes the current, making hash of the sea, and we fly over a swell and thump down in a trough. I say, "This is a bone-rattling ride, and the weather's getting worse. But we've got to stop his boat from running aground."

Silence falls over the cabin as the boat surges over a swell. I bet they're thinking of survival and making it to the marina. A few minutes later, I point to a power boat ahead. "Hold on. This'll get rough."

The man from Shore Lodge groans, and Violet says, "We'll get through this."

I knock on wood and hope she's right.

DEL

My pulse quickens, and my armpits are damp. I grip a handhold tight, smelling fear in my sweat. I bite my lip and hope the staff from Shore Lodge won't commandeer a boat and chase me across the water.

Jacklyn says, "How're you doing? Are you afraid they'll find you?"

I swallow as the boat flies up and thumps down in the waves. I say, "I'm terrified they'll take me back."

Her blue eyes bore into me. "I thought you could check out at any time if you weren't admitted, like I was."

I nod. "I checked myself in, but I was supposed to get medical authorization to leave, which I didn't do."

Karina looks pale and ready to puke. She's staring at the floor. Jacklyn says, "Karina, stare at the horizon, so you won't get sick."

Karina winces. "It's hard to do when we're moving up and down so much."

Jacklyn says to me, "Why'd you want to leave Shore Lodge so much?"

I sigh. "It's a long story. I'll tell you another time."

Violet says, "I'd like to hear it."

Karina just swallows and stares south with a sheen of sweat on her face.

I hope I'll make it through this ordeal and not throw up or be chased down by staff from Shore Lodge. The water is so rough, I'm not sure how Irena will be able to pull this off.

JACKLYN

My stomach knots at the idea of seeing Dusty, who issued a distress call. I wonder if he's really in trouble and if it's another cry for attention. But then I see his boat drifting, heading right for a dock by the two refineries outside of town, where nature butts up against commerce, and I know this is a real emergency. Normally the refinery smokestacks belch out swirls of vapor, forming clouds, but today dark storm clouds cover the sky.

I gulp, picturing Dusty's boat ramming the oil refinery dock and causing an oil slick or an explosion. I say to Irena, "He's headed right for the refinery dock."

"Yep, but we'll get there first, if I can help it." She pushes on the throttle and the boat surges ahead, bouncing over three-foot waves.

She says, "Here we go. Hold on."

VIOLET

I press my lips together and hold on tight as the boat fights its way through choppy seas. Irena is steady at the helm as we head south in the storm to rescue a stranded boater. The fact that the boater is Jacklyn's son is typical of life in a small town, where we're connected in a web of support and idle gossip, depending on the day.

A boat ahead in the bay tosses back and forth, pushed by churning waves and battered by high winds. A tall broad-shouldered man comes out of the wheelhouse and lumbers to the bow, letting out the anchor. He looks toward shore and shakes his head as his boat is shoved toward the refinery dock.

I clear my throat. "He's drifting closer to shore."

Irena says, "He threw out his anchor, but it's not slowing him down much."

I turn to my sister. "Karina, how're you doing?"

She bites her lip. "Okay, I guess. I didn't expect it to be this rough."

"I'm sorry for dragging you into this," Jacklyn says.

The man who joined us from Shore Lodge says, "I'm glad you came to Cedar Island today, or I wouldn't have gotten away. I can never thank you enough."

I nod to him and tighten my grip on the handhold as the bow rears up and comes crashing down. He seems like a nice guy who deserves his freedom, like everyone on board does.

I frown, thinking that Dusty, who we're about to rescue, is another story. He should be locked up for what he did to his mother while she was grieving. He almost got away with selling her house and spending all her money, but she stopped him. Because of that and how she escaped from Shore Lodge, I admire and respect her.

I say to Jacklyn, "You took us on a carnival ride."

She tips back her head and laughs.

I smile and glance at Dusty on his boat as we approach. Part of me wishes he would disappear into the Salish Sea and never darken Jacklyn's door again.

39

KARINA

I rest a hand over my queasy stomach and stare at the refinery, which is growing closer, and wonder how we'll manage to rescue Jacklyn's son before he smashes into the pier. A huge tanker is docked there, maybe taking on fuel. What a disaster it'll be if Dusty rams the dock, ruptures a pipeline, or slams into the ship.

Del says, "This looks bad. Are we going to hit the pier?"

In a calm voice, Irena says, "Not on my watch."

I gaze at the roiled gray water and think about the birds, seals, fish, whales and other sea life that will be hurt or die in an oil spill. I say, "So, there's a chance we'll get there in time before he slams into the ship?"

"You bet," she says. "I'll come in on his port side, the one closest to us, lash the boats together and steer him away from the refinery pier and tanker. I'll tow him into the marina, where he can get a diver to inspect the prop and cut off the line he likely picked up. Okay, it's go-time. Jacklyn and Violet, drop the fenders on both sides of the boat and hold on tight. It's going to get rough."

I'm best suited to baking scones and brewing coffee than helping on a boat, but I say in a shaky voice, "Can I do something?"

"Keep a lookout for other boats and call out the distance to the dock. Okay, Violet and Jacklyn, go." Jacklyn and Violet step outside, holding on to hand rails and dropping fenders over the sides. A large wave rears up and crests over the bow, washing over the windshield and blocking our vision for a moment.

I hold my breath and hope nothing will happen to my two friends out on deck. While the wiper blades clear the windshield, Violet and Jacklyn make their way back to the cabin. I shiver, thinking how cold they must be.

Irena says. "Karina, how close are we to the dock? Count off for me."

I snap out of my musings and stare to the south. "We're about a block from the dock right now."

"Keep watch for me. Call it out."

Jacklyn and Violet enter the cabin and shut the door, closing out the noise of the churning sea and howling wind. They're chuckling and slapping high fives as if they just has the most amazing adventure, but their clothes are sopping wet.

Irena says, "Thanks for doing that. I'll tie up on his port side and tow him away from danger."

She grabs her phone and calls Dusty, who answers right away, and she tells him her plan. She listens as he says something, and she says, "Good idea about the anchor. When I come alongside and lash the boats together, I want you haul up the anchor right away. I don't want to get the chain wrapped around my prop."

He says something else, and she shakes her head. "The anchor did its job and slowed you down. But as soon as I set up for a tow, I'll need that anchor onboard your boat."

She listens for a moment and says into the phone, "Listen, I'm rescuing you, and we'll do it my way. See you soon."

She hangs up and says, "He's a stubborn one, isn't he?"

Jacklyn nods and grimaces. "He's been that way since he was little."

I stare out a salt spray covered windshield and say, "Half a block from the refinery dock and closing fast."

40

JACKLYN

Irena slows our speed and swings the wheel, coming alongside the power boat's port side. She says, "Jacklyn, take the helm and hold her steady while I prepare to tow her."

I hurry over, taking the wheel. "Got it, skipper."

Irena strides out to the boat deck and quickly lashes the boats together at midships.

Dusty says something to her before stomping to his bow, screaming into the wind and hauling up his anchor. I shake my head and grip the steering wheel, keeping an eye on the depth finder. Typical of Dusty to have a tantrum when we're going out of our way in a storm to save his sorry butt.

He stomps back to midships and yells something to Irena. His face is flushed, featuring his famous glaring frown. I snap my attention to the dock, which is coming in clearer view, and turn the wheel, taking the boats away from the tanker.

To the north, two tug boats appear out of the gloom, coming toward us. Black smoke billows out of their white smoke stacks. They're pouring it on, probably poised to haul us away to protect the refinery's pipeline and pier, where the tanker is docked.

The marine radio crackles, coming to life. "This is the Coast Guard. Nimbus Boat Rescue, do you require additional assistance at the south end of Fidalgo Bay? Come in please."

Karina says, "The dock is a quarter block away, coming closer."

The two boats bob up and down, shoved by the wind and waves, as we move away from the dock and certain disaster. I grab the marine radio microphone and say in a calm, measured voice, "This is Nimbus Boat Rescue. We have the situation under control. Thank you. Nimbus Boat Rescue over and out."

A blast of cold air from the north pushes our boats back toward the dock.

Karina says in a tight voice, "Getting closer. Collision coming any minute."

Irena hurries inside, water dripping from her rain jacket, and takes the wheel. "Thanks, I'll take it from here."

I scoot over, and Irena says, "No collisions on my watch. Not now or ever."

The two tug boats steam ahead, coming closer.

Silence reigns in the wheelhouse.

She pushes on the throttle, and we slowly move ahead, taking my son's boat with us and leaving the refinery dock behind. I glance behind at our white churning wake and release a sigh.

Irena says, "All clear. You can relax. We're heading to the marina."

"At last," the man from Shore Lodge says, tugging on his ear lobe.

I wipe my moist palms on my khaki shorts. "Thank goodness."

Irena gazes straight ahead and says over her shoulder. "Jacklyn, Dusty said he wants to talk to you. Something about Christmas Eve dinner at your place?"

I let out a groan and roll my eyes. "What part of betrayal doesn't he understand? There'll be no family dinners for him anymore at my house. Not after what he did, sticking me in Shore Lodge."

"Here, here," Del says.

The others cheer, and I smile, letting my rigid shoulders relax. I'm not alone. I have the perfect dog and friends who will back me up, defending me to my last breath. Life doesn't get better than that.

41

JACKLYN

We turn toward the marina, towing the other boat alongside, and I glance into my son's boat. He's standing at the helm, hands on the wheel, despite his boat having lost power, and staring straight ahead. Boating brings us humble pie when we least expect it, and he was served a lesson in humility today. Everything's going along fine and then, wham, you're in dire straits due to weather, or taking evasive action when a boat headed your way doesn't yield or follow the time-worn rules of the sea. Albert and I were boating once when a yacht glided toward us on a collision course, going twenty knots. Even though we had the right of way, the boat kept coming, so we turned away, and it chugged by on autopilot with no skipper at the helm. We hailed the skipper on the marine radio and got no reply. Albert and I wiped our brows and shook our heads at our close call.

Now, I let out a sigh and know I'll always miss Albert, but life moves on. I have a new life, and it's up to me how I spend my time left. I glance at Irena, Violet and Karina and nod to them. I'm fortunate to have these women in my life.

The boats, bound at midships, plow through choppy seas. A gust of wind pushes us toward the refinery dock, and Irena clenches her jaw as she steers. I say to her, "Everything okay?"

She shrugs. "We'll make it, but the storm is building, and the barometer's dropping."

Wind whines, sending a chill up my spine. I shiver and say, "Not the best day to be boating."

Karina half-smiles. "You can say that again. What I wouldn't give for a hot cup of coffee right now."

Irena nods and heads for the marina breakwater. "I'll take a gallon of coffee after this."

"Amen to that," Violet chimes in. "And a boatload of warm clothes and scones."

Del grins. "I'm hungry, now that you mention it. Can we stop and eat at the café after this?"

Karina shivers. "I don't see why not."

Violet asks, "Do you have to check Dusty's propeller first?"

"Nope, not my job. I just tow them to safety and it's up to someone else to fix it."

I smile and out of the corner of my eye, catch Dusty staring and glowering at me. He sure knows how to hold a grudge of his own making. Goosebumps prick my flesh at the sight of my son despising me for no reason, except that he feels entitled to every bit of my money and my home. He wants them for his benefit, even though that would put me out on the streets.

I shake my head and scowl at him through the salt-crusted windows. He's my flesh and blood, and although I birthed him, he lost his family status when he sold my garden store and stole my meaning and purpose, revealing a greed-centered self.

"Prepare to dock," Irena says, pulling me out of my pit of despair and distraction. There's no need to linger on what's wrong. I'll remain upbeat and positive. That's what I've learned from my time behind closed doors at Shore Lodge. Never give up, stay positive and keep a mindset of driving toward a goal of some sort, even if it is reading one book a month.

A broad smile breaks out across my face because I'm going to grab all the life I can and learn new skills. I'll build a subdivision on the hill above town with beautiful homes. That'll be my contribution to town and my driving force, after my son snatched away my garden store. I'll bloom in a new place, and Dusty can't stop me.

42

DUSTY

My boat bucks the waves, tethered to Irena's, and I slam a fist on the helm. If Mom was nicer to me and told me where she was going, I could've taken her there. Then we'd have dinner at her house, with her cooking for me. I like how she makes turkey stuffing, not how it comes from a box. My mouth waters, and I imagine a roast turkey on the table with a pan of moist stuffing, a pitcher of brown gravy and her creamy green bean casserole. It wouldn't take her long to prepare it. But what am I thinking? She won't even talk to me. Our relationship is ruined, and I don't see a way back.

My stomach growls, and I hold on as a huge wave rears up and crashes on the foredeck. The boats surge over a swell, and my hull hums, the boat deck vibrating under my feet.

I grit my teeth and hold on as we head for the marina. I shake my head, searching for someone other than my mother to blame for my predicament. In the back of my mind, I know it's my fault because I had no business going out on a day like this during a storm, despite small craft warnings. But I'll never admit that to anyone. Blame is my business, and it's what I do best.

I glance into Irena's boat and squint at my mother, who is smiling at something someone said. Sure, leave it to her to be happy-go-lucky when I'm in a tough situation. She doesn't care. I'll pay her back for that. I'm not sure how, but I'll think of a way.

43

DEL

The boat lurches, and I hang on as waves smack the side of the boat, tossing sea spray into the air. I frown and recall running from Shore Lodge and following Jacklyn and her friends down to the dock. At home, I'd been sad and teary-eyed about retiring, rattling around with little to do, so I admitted myself to Shore Lodge's first floor. The others on this boat wouldn't understand because they're younger and driven, not knowing what lies ahead on the road to aging.

I clear my throat. "Jacklyn, when you escaped from Shore Lodge, you were an inspiration to me, and when I saw you leaving the building earlier today, I followed you."

She beams, blue eyes twinkling. "I'm glad I was a source of inspiration."

"You must miss owning your garden store. I know I miss working."

"When I got out, I took over my son's construction company, and that's a new challenge. It's pretty bad when you can't trust your own family member, isn't it?"

Violet says, "It's more common than you might expect."

Karina sighs. "I can't wait until we're back on land drinking coffee."

The breakwater for the marina appears ahead, and a gust of wind bears down.

Jacklyn says, "It must be blowing thirty knots, don't you think?"

Irena nods. "Definitely not a good day to be boating and lose your power. I'll drop Dusty's boat at his slip before we go to mine. From there, we'll head to the café."

She expertly nudges the other boat into a slip and says to Dusty, "You'll have to get a hold of a diver to check your prop. Give me your credit card number now, so I can bill you."

His face flushes, and he puts his hands on his hips, frowning. A vein throbs in his forehead. He says, "You can't do that. I don't have my credit card with me, so just send me a bill. You've got to take care of my prop now."

"I'm just responsible for the tow. The rest is your responsibility. You're lucky I was available to tow you in, and you didn't crash onshore or into the dock."

He splutters. "If you're going to charge me, the least you could do is to dive down and fix it now."

Irena shrugs. "I'm taking the rest of the day off and tomorrow. End of story."

She comes in the wheelhouse and drives her boat slowly away. Dusty yells, cupping his hands, and shakes a fist. Irena says, "Everyone thinks they're special. But I need a day off, especially on a holiday."

"Darn right," Jacklyn says, patting her on the back. "I agree. Don't bend to his will. I coddled him too much when he was young."

Irena backs into her slip, and Jacklyn hops off the boat, tying the dock lines. We step down on the dock and the wind carries snow flurries flying past. I zip my jacket and stomp my feet for warmth while Irena shuts down the engine and checks the lines. She says, "We made it home, which I call it a huge success."

I say, "Hats off for saving me and rescuing Dusty. Well done."

Jacklyn says, "Who's ready for a gallon of hot coffee before I go home and see my sweet dog?"

"And scones," Violet says. "Karina, okay if we take over your café?"

She smiles. "You bet. Come to my place. It'll be on the house. I'm just glad to be back on dry land."

"Can I come along too?" I say. "I don't have anywhere to go. I've been living full-time at Shore Lodge on the first floor for a while."

"Of course," Karina says. "The more the merrier, especially after what we just went through. That was a bonding experience."

Walking down the dock, I struggle to keep up with the four women striding along. Jacklyn says to me, "I'll give you a ride in my car. We'll talk on the way to the restaurant. I want to hear more of your story."

I cringe. What drove me to seek shelter for a time at a facility on Cedar Island feels private and personal and not something I want probed or discussed with strangers, not even with Jacklyn, who lived there for a brief time. I'll have to gather my courage and tell her I don't want to talk about it.

A squad car from the Millersville Police pulls up, blocking our path, and two officers get out. A middle-aged woman with short hair says, "Are you Del Witherspoon?"

My chest grows tight, and I say, "Yes."

"Authorities at Shore Lodge say you escaped, and they asked us to detain you until they can pick you up and take you back."

I swallow. "I voluntarily admitted myself, and I left on my own accord. I'm not going back." Out of the corner of my eye, I see Jacklyn fiddling with her phone.

An older officer with a beer-belly adjusts his cap and eyes me. "Are you sure about that? Nurse Wright and Dr. Henderson, who are donors to our annual gala, tell us you were unduly influenced by Jacklyn Stone."

The middle-aged officer looks at the group of women who saved me. "Which one of you is Jacklyn Stone?"

Jacklyn steps forward. "That's me."

"They said you were a trouble maker and to bring you in on charges of disturbing the peace. You two, come with us."

Jacklyn holds up her phone. "We won't be going anywhere. Fred, are you getting this?"

"Yes, I heard all that and recorded it to use in court. Let me speak with the officers."

They glance at each other and shrug, stepping to the phone.

"I'm Jacklyn Stone's attorney and she has done nothing wrong. Let them go home now, and we'll come down to the police station in the morning to get this all sorted out. I don't care if the administrators at Shore Lodge contributed to the annual ball. Their influence should have no weight in this matter."

The two officers step to the side, talk for a few minutes and come over to us. The older man says, "You're free to go about your business. Have a good evening, and if I were you, I'd avoid stepping foot in Shore Lodge in the future. If you do, things might not go as well the next time."

Jacklyn nods and says, "Thank you, and Merry Christmas." As we walk away, she says into her phone, "Thanks, Fred. See you in a bit. We appreciate the help."

She turns to me and says, "Talk about a fruit basket

upset back there, but we caught a break and escaped from the long reach of Shore Lodge."

I stop and bend over, hands on my knees. "I wasn't sure what was going to happen. I could barely breathe when I thought they'd take me back there."

She smiles. "Not this time, not on my watch."

We climb in her car, and she drives out of the marina parking lot, with the windshield wipers moving, clearing fast-falling snow. She says, "Why did Nurse Wright and Dr. Henderson chase after you, if you admitted yourself to the first floor? Shouldn't it be okay for you to leave?" She glances over and eyes me with piercing blue eyes.

I take a deep breath and slowly let it out. It feels like safe territory, talking about the facility and not my personal problems, which would be too much for me to share at this point. I say, "That's what I thought, but they were resistant to letting me go. When I checked myself in, I assumed I could leave when I wanted."

Jacklyn turns the wheel, rounding a corner, and she cackles. "I call him Dr. Goatee, the administrator. I thought he ran a good group session on the first floor. But he and Nurse Wright were certainly intense gate keepers, stopping me from leaving."

I say, "Despite the money spent, I have to admit they helped me come to terms with a problem I was having. I'm glad I went there. I just don't understand why they wouldn't let me leave."

She pulls over, parks outside Gigi's Café and turns to

me. "Whatever was bothering you, there's no need to tell me about it. I respect your privacy. Believe me, I've been through dark times and wondered if I'd ever see light on the other side of the long tunnel."

A weight lifts from my chest, and I look out the side window, wiping a tear from my eye. I gather my courage to expose my innermost thoughts, wounds and worries, and turn to look at her. "I never expected retirement to be a hole I stepped into, a void with no meaning. I'm not needed anywhere. Sure, I have time on my hands to do what I want, but I don't have hobbies, because I was working all the time."

She faces forward and says, "I know what you mean. When my son sold my garden store, I thought where's my meaning and purpose? Why go on living if I'm not needed anywhere? Who am I without my store and my work?" She blows out a breath and continues. "But I found something else to do that interests me and offers new challenges every day, and that works for me. Change is difficult, and no one likes it. I had to shrug off my defeatist attitude, like a heavy coat that doesn't fit anymore, and move on."

I chuckle. "Retiring for me was like putting on a bathrobe that was two sizes too big. I was overwhelmed with choices and didn't know what to do with my time. I can't tell you how many people told me to get a dog, so I'd have to take it for walks."

She looks at me and smiles. "I don't know where I'd be

without my dog, Buddy. He brought me through tough times after my husband passed away, on our wedding anniversary, no less."

"I'm sorry to hear that about your husband. Here I am whining about not working, but you lost a loved one."

She says, "Let's grab some coffee and scones. Karina's food makes everyone feel better."

I get out of the car and, as we hurry inside, say, "I'll think about getting a dog."

I don't tell her as she marches ahead, bracing against the wind, but my brother caused my wife's death, and for that, I can't forgive him. That's what drove me to go to Shore Lodge.

44

NURSE WRIGHT

Standing on the roadside, I stamp a foot and clutch a bit of coat fabric in my clenched hands. Jacklyn Stone got away from me again. She bested me twice and made me look bad in front of my boss.

I grimace and squint as wind flings grit in the air. A tree branch cracks, falling with a thud. Tiny snowflakes swirl past. This should be a peaceful scene, but my acidic gut tells me otherwise.

Doctor Henderson tugs on his goatee and glares. "This is all your fault."

I cock my head and rest my hands on my hips. No way I'll carry the blame about a first-floor resident running off, leaving an empty room without a body on the wait list to fill the bed and pay the bills. I clear my throat and say,

"I'm in charge of the second floor, not the first. If you give me a promotion and a big raise, I'd be happy to run both."

His eyes grow wide. "We don't have the budget to give you a raise."

I point at him. "Then the first floor is your responsibility, and yours alone."

He runs his hands over his face. "How did this happen?"

I cross my arms. "I can think of a few things that might've led to his leaving. You raised the rates, almost doubling the fees."

"We had to. Costs were going up. The minimum wage increased."

I snort and say, "Not by that much. I'd say you and the board got greedy."

He barely nods, looking down at a pothole in the paved, cracked road.

I'm just getting started, so I continue. "You laid off the chef and went with a newbie who barely knows her way around the kitchen. The food quality went down. Even residents on my floor are complaining about how bland the food is, and the oatmeal is watery. Can't you do better than that? Families were willing to pay more when they saw the quality of the food. But not anymore."

He opens his hands. "I have to show a profit to the board. I can't please everyone."

My cheeks ache from the cold, and I say, "Dollar signs turned your head around, and you're not seeing straight.

The most important stakeholders are the families paying for residents' care and guests shelling out for themselves on the first floor. They care about the level of service and food quality. If we lose more residents, word will get around, like it did after Jacklyn Stone escaped. And while you're at it, hire better people. You've been laying off seasoned employees and taking on kids fresh out of high school."

He groans. "I have to watch the bottom line."

"Take a longer-term view, otherwise Shore Lodge will close and we'll be looking for work.

He says, "Food for thought. Thanks for your honest input."

"There's more where that came from."

"I have no doubt of that." He turns to his car, climbs in and rolls down the window as snowflakes swirl past. A gust of wind pushes me, and I brace myself. He says, "Take the rest of the day off."

"That's what I was doing before you called. I haven't had a day off in months."

He waves and drives off in a cloud of diesel exhaust, and I cough. Although it's my day off, I'll stop in at Shore Lodge to see how it's going. The charge nurse I hired is unsure of herself. I'll pop by and conduct a surprise inspection before heading home. That will keep my staff on their toes.

45

DUSTY

I climb in my truck and step on the gas, following my mother from the marina to Gigi's Café. When she parks, I pull over and drum on the steering wheel, considering what to do. I'm hungry and low on funds. Somehow I'll have to come up with the money to pay my credit card balance, which now has a charge from Nimbus Boat Rescue. I'll call the credit card company to dispute Irena's charge and say she didn't carry out the full scope of work.

My mom and an older guy get out of her car and go inside the café. I slam down a fist on my cracked dashboard. Ever since she came back from Shore Lodge, everything's been going wrong for me.

A couple walks by, bracing against the wind, and they look over at me, eyebrows raised, like I'm an oddball with a problem. I slide out of the truck, stride toward the café and mutter to myself, "Nothing's wrong with me. Is everyone an idiot in this town?"

I shove the screen door open, and it slams shut behind me. People in the café stop talking and turn to me, looming large in the doorway. I grit my teeth and gently close the wooden front door, so it clicks shut with a snick.

Scanning the room, I spot my mother with the man she came in with, Irena, and Violet, who looks like someone you shouldn't mess with. My mom raises her eyebrows and locks eyes with me. Violet crosses her arms, narrows her brown eyes and cocks her head. Karina ignores me, bustling past carrying a pot of coffee. She didn't even bother to say hello, which ticks me off.

I stride over to the table where my mother is sitting and slam my fist on the table. Metal utensils clatter, and coffee cups rattle. Everyone flinches, especially Mom, which makes me feel good. Her blue eyes flick away from mine, like she's afraid, which is exactly what I'm aiming for.

I say to her, "I'm hungry and out of money, and it's your fault. You took what was mine. You should invite me to dinner tonight, because we're family, and it's a tradition."

My mom stands and meets my gaze. "I don't know what planet you're on, but after what you did to me, you're out of my will and my life. We're not family anymore. Family members don't betray each other and stick a grieving loved one in a psych ward."

I grab her cup, gulp hot coffee and it burns on the way down. "I'll take three scones and slices of quiche to go," I tell Karina when she appears with the coffee pot. "Put it on my mother's tab. She owes me."

Mom says, "Take your anger and get out of here." She makes a shooing motion, like I'm a stray cat. "Go on. You need help. Get counseling and stop blaming everyone but yourself."

I plant my legs apart and slam the coffee mug down on the table. They all jerk, which makes me smile. I'm not powerless, they are. "I'll leave when I want to."

Karina's face flushes, and she holds the coffee pot between us, pointing to the door with her free hand. "Your mother's right. Go on, get out of here or I'll have you trespassed from the premises. You'll have that on your police record. How would you like that?"

I clear my throat. "Idle threats. You wouldn't do that, not to the son of someone you know."

"Believe me, I will," Karina says.

I say, "You look cute when you're angry. Has anyone ever told you that?"

She rolls her eyes and moves away. Violet, who is built like she lifts weights, stands and steps forward, pointing a finger at my chest. "Like my sister said, leave before she calls the cops."

I chuckle. "Or what? You'll make me?"

Mom says, "You're making a scene, Dusty. Please leave. We did nothing to incur your wrath."

I scowl. "Now you're using fancy language? Why don't you just come right out and say what you mean? You don't love me and never did. My sister is your favorite, and you showed it every day when I was growing up. Then she had a baby, and you were all over that, talking about your grandson every chance you could. Because of you, no one in town will hire me, and I had to move away. It's your fault I live in a moldy cabin far from anywhere."

"Stop playing the victim," Mom says, shaking her head. "Grow up and take responsibility for your life. It's not too late."

"Dad helped me when I needed it. Why won't you chip in?"

Mom sighs and glances around the café, where people are watching us and listening to every word. Mr. Frackus, my high school science teacher, stands at the front counter cocking his head and scrutinizing me, as if he's disappointed in me.

Mom says, "It's your life, and you get to decide how to live it. But I have one important thing to say, and it's for you to stop mooching and grow up. So what if you live in an old cabin in the middle of nowhere? Get a job and save, so you can move to a better place."

It looks like there's no chance of her taking pity and giving me money, so I put my hands together and make a final plea. "It's not that easy. You could at least make me dinner every night, so I'd have one good meal a day. That's what a good mother would do." I turn to the rapt audience in the café. "Don't you agree? She's my mother. Shouldn't she cook for her son?"

A woman with dark curly hair and her table-mate, who is wearing a gaudy pink workout outfit, shake their heads and focus their attention on two books on the table. I glare and scan the room, but no one meets my gaze.

Someone whispers, "What a jerk."

Another says in a low voice, "He certainly thinks well of himself."

"He's unhinged, for sure."

A heavy weight is on my heart, reminding me of when I was young. I'm alone and alienated, licking childhood wounds I've tried to forget. I rest a hand on my stomach and moan. "I'm in pain, all the time. I didn't want to tell you, Mom, but I've been diagnosed with a rare disease. That's why I can't work. I need your help. I'm your son. Don't turn me away."

I lean a hand on the table and blink hard, squeezing out a few tears, letting them dribble down my cheeks. I've been practicing this in my moldy digs to be prepared for a performance and tap into her sympathy on an occasion like this, when I'm out of options to make things go my way. Mom purses her lips and looks out the window, so I don't think she's buying my act.

An older man with big ears clenches his fists and says, "Don't speak to your mother like that. Give her the respect she deserves. You should be ashamed of yourself for selling her store."

I snort. "You can huff and puff all you like but don't get between my mother and me. You don't know what's going on, Pops, so butt out."

Karina comes up to me, trying to tell me off, but I brush off her comments. This is between my mother and me, and other people shouldn't butt in. I'm a grown man, and Karina can't tell me how to act.

A police officer comes in the café, hitching up her pants and looking around. She asks Karina, "Is this man giving you trouble?"

Karina, Violet, Irena, Mom, the older guy and the two book lovers all say, "Yes."

"You'll have to vacate the premises," the officer says, coming over and walking me toward the door.

People in the café clap as I'm paraded to the door by the officer. My face heats. Smearing guilt didn't work, so I'll have to come up with another angle for manipulating my mother's emotions.

I turn around and say in a loud voice, "I need money to go to the tavern and hang out with friends. And Irena, I want my boat repaired now. I'm a priority customer."

Mom cups her hands and says, "You're thirty-one. Grow up and get a job."

I glare into the café before crossing the threshold and say, "Just you wait. I'll be back."

"No, you won't," says the officer.

Karina says, "You're not welcome here anymore."

46

KARINA

Bernard Frackus, my grandmother's secret boyfriend who works for me, stands at the front counter in the café. We lock eyes, raise our eyebrows and listen to Dusty complain in a loud voice about the state of his life. He makes it sound like it is everyone else's fault, but I happen to know from his mom that he's made questionable money choices. He may think he's Teflon, walking around with a no-fault sign on his back, but it's time he grew up and took responsibility for his life. I should know, because I had to smooth out wrinkles in my world when my grandmother died.

I move over to Bernard and say in a low voice, "I'll call the cops." I slip into the kitchen and make the call, saying I need someone trespassed from my business, before slipping back into the café. I pause at the counter by Bernard, and we take in Dusty's tirade at his mother and the world in general. His main complaint is about how he's down and out and not getting help from her or invites to meals. A lot of fun he'd be at the dinner table, complaining and frowning.

I whisper to Bernard, "Hold off serving food until we get Dusty out of here. I'm going to tell him off for coming in and disrupting my business."

I clear my throat and open my mouth to say something to Dusty just as he turns to me, pointing a finger. A vein throbs in his forehead, and his face is beet red. He asked me out a while back, but I turned him down. No way I'd go out with a grown man-child who throws tantrums in public and blames his mother for his problems.

Dusty says, "What're you talking about? You should just shut up."

I cross my arms and shrug, pretending he can't get under my skin, but I'm rattled by his seething anger. I want him out of the building, so he'll stop bothering my customers, and my café will go back to being a feel-good place.

I point to the door. "Dusty, you'd better leave. I called the cops."

He puts his hands on his hips and glares, but I stare back at him, standing my ground. "This is my business and you can't come in and make a scene. Go on, get out, and don't come back. And leave your poor mother alone. You crushed her soul, tricking her to go to Shore

Lodge and admitting her. It's a black mark on your soul."

Everyone in the café claps, and he storms toward me, red-faced with beads of sweat on his brow. He says, "I'll go where I like when I like. You're not the boss of me."

A police officer strides in, scanning the room. I wave to her, and she looks at me, saying, "Is this man bothering you?"

I nod. "Yes."

The officer says to Dusty, "Come with me, and don't come back to this business."

As the officer marches him to the door, Dusty snarls at his mom, but she dishes it right back to him. The screen door slaps shut, and the café is quiet. I let out a loud whoosh of breath, and Jacklyn cheers and claps. We all join in, and I say, "Good riddance to him." I turn to Bernard and say, "Let's get those orders for scones and quiche served."

He smiles and adjusts his black-rimmed glasses. "I'm on it, boss."

As I serve coffee to customers, one particularly good-looking guy at a window table who happens to be married says, "Quite the scene just now. I was ready to jump up and cart him out the door, but I figured it's your business. Next time, if it happens again, I'm your man if you'd like help."

I smile. "Thanks, Flash. I appreciate that. Back in

Gigi's day, I doubt she needed muscle to manage her business."

He shakes his head. "Times have changed. People like that grow ruder every day."

I tilt my head. "I want Gigi's Café to be a feel-good safe zone, free from nasty remarks and social sniping. I should put a sign in front that says, "Leave the negativity at the door. Come enjoy a positive-only environment with a fresh-baked scone and a cup of strong coffee."

He smiles, flashing a dimple in his cheek. "I like that. I say go for it."

47

JACKLYN

Dusty is escorted out of the café, and I blow out a breath, sinking down into a chair. My neighbor Bernard Frackus sets plates with warm scones and piping hot slices of quiche before us, and my mouth waters. I tell him thanks, and he smiles.

Before I eat, I check my phone for messages, and my mouth drops open. The city planning department emailed to say I must now submit an environmental survey before they'll approve my building permit. I glare at the door and suspect my son is behind this new development. He'd be happy to slow my project and bring me down to regain control of his company.

Swallowing a scalding sip of coffee, I set down the cup. I'll swing by the city planning office on the way home to straighten this out. An environmental survey will not only delay the project but add thousands of dollars to an already hefty budget. Thanks a lot, Dusty. I bet you're working behind my back, slithering around like a snake.

Violet turns to me. "What's wrong?"

"The city added a step to the process before they'll approve my permit, which means more money and a delay getting started breaking ground."

Violet places a warm hand on mine and looks me in the eye. "Are you sure you should be doing this? From what I hear, building a subdivision has a steep learning curve. It might be expensive to learn on the job. Are you sure you don't want Dusty as your advisor? I know he can be a jerk and he has a temper, but he knows building codes and the city planners, from what I hear."

"I don't want my son anywhere near this subdivision. He may know people and the process, but he'd rip me off without blinking an eye. I'm won't set myself up as his victim a second time. I learned my lesson at Shore Lodge."

She shrugs and eats a bite of quiche. "It's up to you. This is so good. I'm going to wolf it down and go to the office before I head home."

I tuck into my food, but the scone and quiche aren't quite as tasty as when I usually come to Gigi's Café. My tastebuds have soured from having a looming fight on my hands with City Hall.

48

VIOLET

I drum my fingers on the café table as we wait for food to be served and tap a toe with nervous energy. I'm wired with adrenaline coursing through my veins after our extraction mission. That was a close call at the dock on Cedar Island.

Karina and Bernard are hustling at top speed, so I get up to offer to help. I go up to Karina, who is talking with a customer and pouring coffee, and tap her on the shoulder. She looks around and smiles at me, and a warm feeling of being loved by my sister spreads across my chest.

I say, "Do you want some help?"

She grins. "Sure, we're swamped. So many people wanted to eat while we were gone that Bernard kept the café open. Why don't you top up coffees? I'll get the food out."

I go around chatting it up with locals and tourists who

are in town for a few days. As I move through the room, I'm reminded of how I want to model my interactions with others based on how Karina treats the world. She wants to make people feel better about themselves when they leave her café, so I look for something positive to say to each person. Perhaps my half-sister and I can change the world, one meaningful interaction at a time.

When the coffee pot is empty, I brew a fresh pot, like Karina taught me, by grinding the beans a bit extra. I push the button and get the pot brewing just as she swings by and stops in her tracks.

She thrusts her hands on her hips and says, "Can you believe what Dusty did? Marching in here like he owned the place and taking over, ranting at Jacklyn that way? I was ready to pop him in the nose."

My hands clench. "I wanted to deck him but decided this is your place, so it should be your call how to handle it."

She pats my shoulder. "Next time, feel free to step in. You're the expert. You're trained in martial arts and subduing people who are making trouble."

I say, "You've got it. If there is a next time, which I hope there won't be."

"Me too. Now let's get more of that jam we made on the tables. People are asking for it."

49

IRENA

I squirm in my seat, sip coffee and listen to Jacklyn talk about her problem with the city planning department. Setting the cup down, I chew on my lower lip and worry about my recent rash decision to take on a silent partner for my business. What was I thinking? I rushed in and threw away my hard-fought for independence in a flash decision to save my ex-husband from a debt collector who is now in prison.

I sigh and stare at the table. My new business partner wants to get together to write up a business plan with revenue forecasts, and she says she wants me to stick to it. I'd rather get a root canal or run up on a rock outside Prevost Harbor.

I text my daughter Kelly to see if she wants me to bring home scones and quiche, but she doesn't answer. She must be busy hanging out with a friend, like she mentioned in a text. I sigh and feel a tug toward home. I'll celebrate success with my friends, gulp down food and get out of here as fast as is polite. Kelly might not want to spend the rest of the afternoon with me, but I can't wait to see her and cook salmon broccoli rice bowls for dinner with sprigs of fresh holly on the table.

I shiver when someone opens the door and cold air rushes inside. Pulling the hood of a rain coat down, her brown eyes lock with mine, and I break out into a wide grin. I wave to my best friend and point to the table. "Abby, come join us."

She comes over, gives me a hug and slides a chair next to me. "I can't stay long. I left Jack alone with the dog. I just popped in for scones and quiche to take home."

I say, "How's he doing?"

Jacklyn leans over. "Yes, how is he?"

Abby's lips thin, and she nods before responding, like she's thinking over her answer. "I'll be honest with you. He has good days and not-so-good days. He still has headaches, but they're not as bad."

"That's tough," I say. Jacklyn chimes in, "It sure is. It's amazing he's alive after what Buzz did to him."

Abby brightens, and her eyes shine. I can see why Jack fell in love with her. She's smart and generous and kind, the best parts of a human packaged into one remarkable person who knows how to invest in the stock market while working at an ice cream factory. Her brown hair shimmers under the café lights, and her cheeks are rosy. Being in love with Jack looks good on her. I say, "Has he shown any signs of wanting to buy expensive sneakers again? Is he missing the ones we sold to get him out of debt?"

She shakes her head. "No, he hasn't. I'm keeping him too busy to think about it. We walk our dog three times a day."

Jacklyn raps the table. "Good for you. Buddy would agree with that. If I let him, he'd spend all day sniffing a clump of grass on the corner, where all the dogs stop."

Abby stands and says, "See you around. I need to pick up my order and get home."

"Wait," I say, reaching out. "Did Kelly come over to your place? She's not answering my texts."

Abby tilts her head, gazing at the ceiling. "No, we invited her over, but didn't hear back."

I frown, wondering why Kelly has gone radio silent, but then chide myself for worrying too much. She probably has her head phones on, listening to music. Or her friend is over, and she left her phone in the other room.

At the counter, Karina hands Abby a bag that looks heavy. Abby takes it, waves to us and sweeps out the door.

Jacklyn says, "Isn't that something? Those two found love after all these years. The party's never over until the music stops and dirt's thrown on the coffin."

I gaze out the window, thinking about Buzz, my former boyfriend, and how he hid secrets from his closest friends. Guilt ate him alive from the inside.

Jacklyn pats my hand. "Are you thinking about Buzz?"

I nod. "He had a dark side I didn't know about."

Jacklyn cocks her head. "Maybe we all do. Take my son, for instance, he's got a dark side that he's not hiding anymore. He's flaunting it and has lost his self-control."

I say, "He sounded desperate when he was here and unleashed, like nothing was holding him back. Maybe you taking away his development project undid him, leaving the angry, verbally abusive parts for us to see."

She nods. "Could be."

Karina and Bernard set down plates with scones and slices of quiche. "Here's your food. Sorry it took so long."

I point to my plate. "Thanks, but I ordered two scones, not one."

Karina shrugs. "We're sold out. Abby took the last ones, and this late in the day on Christmas Eve, we're going to close up soon. So, I won't be cooking more, sorry."

I give her a warm smile. "You need to celebrate with Violet and your friends, and I need to go home to Kelly. Did you get my order to go ready?"

Her eyes grow wide, and she opens her hands. "Oh, no. I completely forgot. I'm so sorry."

I stand and say, "That's okay. It's been a long day, and it isn't even over. I'll just take this home, and we'll share it."

Karina wraps it up and a few minutes later, I'm walking out the door after saying goodbye to my friends who are my newfound family. I pause at the door, holding the take-out bag in my hand, and gesture like a homecoming queen to the crowd. "Goodbye. Have a Merry Christmas snug inside, away from the storm."

Jacklyn grins. "And a Merry Christmas to you and Kelly!"

I head home and wonder what I'll find there. I hope my detestable dad won't be lurking outside my house, or hanging out with Kelly, despite my warning him to stay away from us. I clench my jaw and drive, making a wish for a cozy evening at home with peace, harmony and goodwill and no phone calls from the Coast Guard asking me to go out on a wild, windy night to help boaters in distress.

50

—————

NURSE WRIGHT

I drive down the gravel lane and stop in Shore Lodge's parking lot. Twigs, leaves and branches litter the manicured grounds from the storm. I hop out of my car and stride to the entrance. A strong gust of wind blasts down from the north, carrying the smell of salt air and pine needles. Glancing at the upper floor, I tilt my head, noticing many of the lights are off.

I grab the door handle, yank it open and stride inside. Something feels off. My heart races, and I tell myself to calm down. Nothing's wrong. The building isn't burning, and fire trucks aren't here, like the night Jacklyn Stone escaped. Everything is fine. I'll be home in no time at all.

I nod to a man at the reception desk and pause to examine the sign in sheet for visitors. I cock my head, tapping a finger on the most recent page, and say, "Who are these singers who signed in for my floor?"

He tugs on his pony tail and frowns. "I'm not sure. I'm just filling in while Patty's taking a break."

I examine the writing, and a cold feeling of dread creeps over me, making me shiver. Jacklyn Stone was down at the dock, ferrying away our first-floor resident, which will hurt our bottom line. Might she have come here and gone to my floor for some reason?

I bite my lower lip. I don't want that Stone woman anywhere near my floor ever again, stirring up trouble. She's strong for her age, sixty-one, and a rebel. I prefer docile patients who submit to my rules. I spot a name and cock my head, staring at the pony-tailed man at the reception deck. "Someone with the last name of Woodpecker signed in. Woodruff Woodpecker? What kind of joke is that?"

He shrugs and goes back to tapping on a keyboard. "Sorry, I can't help you."

I hurry to the stairwell, charge up the stairs and barge into my unit. My heart is pounding, and my armpits are damp. I'm not dressed for work, this being my day off, and I glance down at my striped red and white leggings under a festive green velvet flared skirt. It might pay dividends for my staff to see me as human. I have a life outside these walls, just like they do.

All is quiet. A tinkle of light laughter comes from the nursing station, and I stride down the hall, my sneakered damp feet squeaking on the linoleum floor. One thing I'll say for the facility where I work is that we keep it spotless.

The walls are white, the atmosphere is stark, but it is clean. You won't find a speck of dirt or dust most days. That's one thing Dr. Henderson does right, managing the cleaning crew.

I pop in at the nursing station, where three staff are gathered with their backs turned to the hall, and rap my knuckles on the desk. No one turns. The new nurse giggles, putting her hand in front of her mouth. I grind my teeth and scan the hall, assessing the havoc wrought in my absence.

Mrs. Skidmore is in restraints in a chair in her room. She's facing the window and singing softly to herself. The overhead light is off in her room, as is true for the other residents.

I clear my throat. The staff on duty don't notice. I bark out, "Blast it all! Pay attention! Why are the lights off, and why is Mrs. Skidmore in her room without supervision?"

The three turn and stare at me, mouths hanging open.

The charge nurse squares her shoulders and says, "It was my idea to keep the overhead lights off and save electricity, and we're going green and saving energy. I thought Mrs. Skidmore would enjoy looking at the view for once."

I glare at her and say, "It's not in your job description to innovate or have ideas. Follow orders and do as you're told, or you'll be back on the ferry without a job in no time."

She half-smiles. "But the ferry isn't running this afternoon because of hazardous wind conditions, so you can't send me home today."

I take a deep breath, telling myself to calm down. It's not like this is an emergency, but I'm making it out to be one. I'm riled up from my run in with Jacklyn Stone, reminding me of my failure to contain her and keep her safe from harm.

I nod to the young woman who recently graduated from nursing school with an attitude of entitlement. I need her working here while I take time off, and no one else applied for the job on our little island, so I'll save my battle for another day, when I'll be on hand and personally train her, molding and shaping her outlook until she is compliant and towing the line, like our residents.

"Point taken," I say. "But please turn on the overhead lights in our residents' rooms. We don't want them stumbling into something and getting hurt. It's not safe, and safety is our top priority. Bring Mrs. Skidmore out to the hall and restrain her in the chair by the nursing station, so you can watch over her. If you don't, as I mentioned before, she'll scratch herself and draw blood, even if her fingernails are trimmed short."

I pause to draw a quick breath, watching for their response. They nod, and I continue. "On the guest sign in sheet downstairs, I saw some singers signed in for our floor. Who are they and what were they doing here? I didn't authorize that visit."

The nurse shrugs. "They were called something like

the Starlight Triplet Singers, and they brought us coffee and scones and quiche."

I narrow my eyes and point to a few dry crumbs on the corner of her mouth. "You have crumbs there on your mouth. You might want to brush them off and present a professional appearance."

The nurse glares at me and swipes a finger across her lips. "They were very nice, and they sang holiday songs for residents in the dayroom."

I put my hands on the desk and lean toward her, trying to get my point across. "We don't let just anyone come in here bringing food without inspecting it first or singing to our people. It could be dangerous."

The three almost roll their eyes, which riles me up even more. My pulse pounds in my ears. "You think I'm exaggerating? Well, I'm not. Anything could happen if you don't keep tight control. These residents need an iron fist in a velvet glove for the floor to run smoothly without disaster occurring. Chaos could reign if you ease up on the pressure and slack off."

An aide pipes up. "Are you talking about when that resident Jacklyn Stone got out? Is that what you mean by disaster? I heard about it, but I didn't work here then."

I gulp. I've backed myself into a corner by eluding to that awful night, which resulted in mountains of paperwork for me to fill out as my penance for letting a patient find a way out on her own. "That's right, that's one example. Now, let's right our ship and tighten adherence to policies and procedures. We know what's best for our residents. Constancy is key to a calming environment. Don't get creative or experiment."

The young nurse crosses her arms and turns up her nose. "I don't feel appreciated. This isn't the job I thought I was being hired for. I don't like how you're speaking to me, and I don't feel respected."

I hold my breath and stop myself from screaming at her, and she glances at the break room door, as if thinking about getting her purse and leaving, which is one thing I don't want. There's no way I want to come into work on Christmas Eve and Christmas day. I hired her as my backup, so I could finally have a holiday with friends and family.

I motion with my hands to simmer down. "I'll be mindful of that in the future. I just stopped in to say Happy Holidays and thank you for being here and taking care of our residents. I really appreciate how you're working today and tomorrow while I'm off."

I give her a warm smile that I hope carries to my eyes, and she gazes at me for a moment, letting her hands drop to her sides. No one else wanted to join me on a remote island managing a secure psychiatric unit, and she apparently needs to hear praise and feel appreciated and respected. It'll be an adjustment for me, but I'll do it.

The young nurse tilts her head and squints, looking about to say something snarky, so I quickly add, "I appreciate you all and Happy Holidays. I'm off."

I tap my badge to a device on the wall, shove open the door and hurry down the stairs. I've never have been one to easily adjust to new conditions. But maybe it is time I treated my employees with more respect. I can grow and learn, like the best of them. If I don't, I may have a mutiny on my hands and end up short-staffed.

51

———

MARY

I stack papers on the desk for residents who want to leave Shore Lodge's secure floor. I turn to my husband and say, "We're as ready as we'll ever be for anyone Jacklyn brings by."

Fred runs a hand through his thinning hair. "It's stormy out. I hope they didn't run into problems."

I pick up my phone and call Jacklyn, but get no answer. Blowing out a breath, I say, "I wonder where they are now. She's been gone a long time since she called you from the marina."

My phone dings with a text, and I glance at it and frown. I say to my husband, "That's odd. Jacklyn says they don't need our help with legal forms."

When I call her, she picks up right away and says in a breathless voice, "I can't talk long. Something's going on with the city planning department. I have to straighten it out right away."

I check the time and see it's past four. "Won't they be closed for the holiday by now?"

"They emailed saying I have to conduct an environmental survey. I can't afford to do that, and I don't want to delay the project. I need to break ground right away."

I hear the sound of a car door slamming and an engine starting in the background. I say, "Come over here and let's discuss it before you charge into the planning office like an angry bull."

"Got to go," she says and hangs up.

I set down my phone, shake my head and say to Fred, "I'd hate to see her ruin her business reputation. She seems to have an undercurrent of anger since she escaped from Shore Lodge."

"As anyone in her position would. Come on, I'll fix you a snack. We can't eat much because we're headed over to Jacklyn's house later."

I leave the blank legal forms on the desk and follow him down the hall to the kitchen. He says, "I'll make a tuna sandwich, and we'll split it."

While he works, I sit at our round kitchen table nursing a hot cup of tea. "I wonder who left from Shore Lodge with Jacklyn. What's their story?"

52

DEL

Jacklyn stands at the café table and says, "Come on, I'll take you home with me. You can stay with my friend Mercury until you're settled. But first we'll make a stop at City Hall."

I swallow and wonder where I'll go after staying with her friend. I gave up my apartment when I moved into Shore Lodge and put my stuff in storage. I say, "I don't want to put anyone out."

She waves it away. "Nonsense. It's no big deal. And you can meet my dog. He's the best rescue pup in the world."

We say goodbye to Irena, Karina and Violet and make our way outside. Grit flies in my face, and leaves dance in the wind. I climb into Jacklyn's car and hope I didn't make a huge mistake by leaving the luxury of Shore Lodge's first floor, where meals are served and linens are changed. My room's view overlooked a meadow and the channel, bringing solace to my soul. I release a slow sigh.

She takes a call and hangs up, starting the car. As she drives, she says, "I'm sorry, I've been wrapped up in my own troubles, when you're fresh from Shore Lodge and you must be mulling over your decision to come with us. Are you having regrets?"

I slowly shake my head. "It's overwhelming and scary, moving to town. I don't have a place to live. I'm retired and don't have a job. My friends are in Seattle."

"I suppose you could move back there."

"Can't afford the city. I've been priced out since my wife and I sold our place and moved north."

"That's too bad." She turns a corner a little too fast for my liking on her mission to correct City Hall. She didn't ask me, but I think she's on a fool's errand to argue with the authorities on the eve of a major holiday weekend. No one wants to listen to outrage or someone complain when they're on the verge of taking time off.

She parks, snugging her tires close to the curb, and says, "How long were you at Shore Lodge?"

"My two-week stay turned into six months. I was dealing with a lot and needed to learn to cope with it."

Resting her hand on the door handle, she gives me a concerned look. "I want to hear more about that, if you want to tell me. But first, let's get this over with."

She marches up to City Hall but stops in her tracks. I get out to see what's going on, and a car backfires, but we ignore it. A notice posted on the glass door says they're closed. She huffs out a breath and turns to me. "Guess I got worked up for nothing. I'll tackle this another day. Let's go home and you can meet my dog and my friend."

As we turn to her car, her son, the tall guy from the café, squats by her rear left tire. Jacklyn runs and stands in front of the tire with her arms stretched out to the sides. She says, "Over my dead body. Go on, get out of here."

I trot over and blurt out, "Stop that right now."

Dusty stands up with a glint in his eye. Gripping a screwdriver, he says, "You should've invited me to dinner, Mother dear." He jogs to a dirty white pickup and takes off in a cloud of exhaust.

Jacklyn puts a hand on the car and coughs. "I think something's wrong with my son. But for years I didn't want to admit it."

I brace against a gust of wind roaring down the road. Sleet stings my face, and white pellets dot the pavement. We inspect her rear tire, and I say, "Looks like we stopped him before he slashed it. How far away do you live?"

She looks west. "About a mile."

"Let's go. I'll keep an eye on it, and the tire places will be closed by now."

Climbing in her car, I shiver and worry about starting a new and better life. I have a feeling my dear departed wife wouldn't like what I did. I buckle up and wipe tears from my eyes as Jacklyn starts the car. She drives through snow flurries, hunched over the wheel and frowning as if the hounds of hell are chasing us down.

53

DUSTY

I jump in my truck, toss the screwdriver inside and stomp on the gas pedal, squealing the tires as I drive off. Glancing in the rear-view mirror, I see my mom bent over coughing.

I wind my way through town, past little houses and boatyards, and merge onto Highway 20, heading east. Mom is tough and doesn't stay down, no matter what I do. I pat my belly and frown at how I'm being deprived of enjoying her holiday dinner with turkey, gravy, stuffing, all the fixings, and chocolate fondue for dessert. She makes the best cocktails, but I won't be having a Manhattan tonight. No Christmas Eve dinner with family is a first for me.

I drive past a church offering a meal with a service and let up on the gas pedal, mulling over whether to stop, but I continue on. I don't want a sermon with a meal. I want my family back, but maybe it's impossible, without Dad here mending the rifts.

I swallow my pride and call my sister, but she doesn't pick up. Snowflakes drift down, and I hang up. My sister is probably with my nephew and friends in Seattle, and she didn't hear the phone ring.

I lean my head against the window and a tear slides down my cheek. I don't understand why everyone turned their backs on me. Anyone else would've done the same thing in my shoes, by admitting Mom to Shore Lodge. She didn't even know her own name at the doctor's office.

I wipe my eyes with the back of my hand and head to a bar on the way to my new digs in a rundown cabin on a rutted dirt road. Maybe I'll find someone to buy me drinks and dinner, given the holiday. I have enough in my wallet for one beer, and my bank account is on life support.

I grit my teeth and park outside Frank's Inn. Stepping out of my truck, I slam the door shut and sniff the cold, damp air, smelling wood smoke. Someone must be having a fire, maybe curled up with a loved one.

I stride to the bar entrance. When word got around Millersville about how I put my mom in Shore Lodge, women stopped speaking to me. It's been the cold shoulder in my hometown. Talk about throwing cold water in an innocent guy's face. Mom's stay at Shore Lodge snapped her out of her grief. I was upset about Dad's death, but I didn't go overboard like she did. I figured we had to get on with our lives and look out for ourselves. That's what Dad would've wanted.

I swing open the bar door and a din of hearty laughter washes over me. I slide onto the last open seat at the bar and lean on my elbows. I'll call this home for tonight until closing, or if I'm lucky, I'll hook up with a tall, long-haired young lady who prefers handsome broad-shouldered guys like me. But my dream bubble bursts when an older grizzled man comes over and says, "That's my seat. Find somewhere else."

I nod and get up, swallowing my pride. There was a time when I would've taken this as an opportunity to vent my anger on a passerby. But I've matured, and I'm above that now. I order a beer and take the can to a spot along the wall, where I lean back and plot and plan how to get back at my mother for abandoning me.

She should ask me to run her company and pay me higher wages for my expertise. I could guide her through the permitting process. I gulp down a slug of beer. I loved her enough to work with healthcare professionals and place her in the best facility in the area. Talk about being ungrateful.

I finish my beer and look around for some chump who might pay for my next one. Wind outside growls, battering the building. A bearded guy in a flannel shirt and jeans at a pool table glances at me and says, "You want in?"

I smile because I've found my mark. "Sure, I don't have the money to bet, though."

54

ROSE

The car ahead on I-5 slows down, and I tap my brakes while reaching over to fling an arm out in front of my son. He's buckled in, but I still worry. Rain drums down, and the wiper blades swish back and forth. I focus on the freeway traffic and hope my mother will be happy to see us when we surprise her.

Max says, "When're we going to get there?"

"Not much longer. We're almost to the turn off for Millersville."

He squirms in his seat. "I'm hungry."

"Eat the granola bar I packed for you."

"I don't want it. I wish Dad was with us. I want Grandma's turkey dinner."

I screw up my face and put the blinker on, taking the exit to Millersville. "I don't think we'll be having a turkey dinner this year. That's why I brought food. She's been keeping to herself since she got home from Shore Lodge. Plus, we're surprising her."

He looks over at me. "We should tell her we're coming. I don't think she likes surprises. She didn't like staying at that creepy lodge." He shivers. "I told you she wouldn't like it."

I bite my lip and stop at a light, recalling how my brother and I tricked Mom into going to a psychiatric treatment center on Cedar Island. I knew he had her durable power of attorney, and I didn't stand up for her in her time of need. I was distracted with parenting Max and my new job in Seattle, so I went along with his plan. But now I realize how wrong I was, and I've been trying to make up for my part in his devious scheme ever since, with frequent calls and visits on weekends whenever I manage to make the drive north to Millersville.

Max says, "She was sad about Grandpa being gone. Uncle Dusty sold her garden store, and that made her even more sad."

I blow out a breath. "You're right, and Dusty shouldn't have done that. It would've been better if she'd stayed home and kept working. But now she has a new project. She's going to build fancy homes on a hill overlooking town."

"Grandma doesn't know about that. She knows about plants. How can she build houses?"

I pat his arm and turn left onto Highway 20, heading

west. "I'm worried about that too. But she'll think of something. She's smart and resourceful."

"Like you."

A tear leaks out of my eye and dribbles down my cheek, and I wipe it away. Max says, "Why are you crying? What's wrong?"

I shake my head and sniffle. "Nothing's wrong. It was sweet what you said. Thanks, buddy."

Rain turns to snow flurries as we head west. My phone rings, and Max looks at it. "It's Uncle Dusty."

My grip tightens on the steering wheel. I've told my brother how wrong it was that he sold our mom's store without her consent and used the proceeds to fund his construction business, but he doesn't see it that way. I say, "Don't answer it. I don't want to talk to him while I'm driving."

He sets the phone down. "Why didn't you invite him to Grandma's for dinner?"

I glance over at an RV park on Padilla Bay. Even though it is late December, every space appears to be taken. "I don't think we're seeing Grandma's situation the same way right now. And Grandma is mad at him for what he did to her."

"You mean that he emptied out her house and was going to sell it?"

I nod. "Yep, that's pretty much it. Maybe one day your uncle and I will agree on something, but right now we're at a stand-off."

"Like in a movie."

Ten minutes later, I pull over and park on the street near the yellow bungalow where I grew up. A blue car is parked right in front of the house, and I wonder whose car it is. As far as I know, my mother hasn't made any new friends.

I get out and go around to help Max, but he opens the door and hops out. The wind plays with his brown hair, making it stand on end for a moment.

I smile and say, "Come on, let's go inside. We'll get the food after we say hello."

We head to the front door, pushing against the wind. Cold biting sleet stings my cheeks, and I pick up my pace. We're almost to my mother's warm home and her welcoming arms. I'll make it up to her someday for what I did, someway, somehow.

55

JACKLYN

I flinch at a loud knock on the door and jump up from the couch, ready to tell Dusty he isn't welcome in my home for the umpteenth time. I'll repeat it until my dying breath, which won't be for a long time. I mulled over the notion of forgiving my son but snipped it in the bud, tossing it in the yard waste of my mind. He's a bad apple and doesn't regret turning my life upside down. There's no forgiving that many wrongs forged by a loved one who has no remorse.

I open the door, forget about my son's thieving treachery and break into a wide smile. My dog lets out a happy bark and runs to my grandson. Max kneels and pets the dog, saying, "Hi, Buddy." They race around the room.

My daughter comes in, bringing a blast of cold air

before I close the door. I give her a hug, and she says, "Max, go play outside if you're going to run around."

He flings open the door and races outside with Buddy, who is barking with joy. Rose closes the door and smiles at me, saying, "I wanted to surprise you."

"And you did. I'm so happy you're here." I open my arms and hug her again, smelling her strawberry-scented shampoo. I step back and smile. "I thought you were staying in Seattle."

She looks around the living room and blinks when she sees my friend Mercury and Del, the man from Shore Lodge. Her jaw drops, but she quickly clamps it shut. Her shoulders sag, as if she came to rescue me from the fate of being a lonely widow suffering alone on a holiday, but now her mission is a bust.

She gazes at me, her eyes filling with tears. "Max and I missed you, and I didn't want you to be lonely on a holiday. But I guess you aren't alone. You have company."

I squeeze her shoulder and gesture to the living room. I'm about to introduce her to the two men when Max and Buddy barge inside, cold air blowing in, and Rose and I say in unison, "Shut the door."

"Sorry," Max says, and runs back to the door, closing it with a thud. Buddy is close on his heels panting. I grab a towel, give Buddy a quick rub down to dry off his coat and toss it aside. Now is not the time to be a fussy neat freak. I want Rose to get to know my visitors and feel at ease in my newly re-decorated home. Dusty cleared it out, tossing my things, before he put it up for sale while I was stashed away conveniently across the channel on Cedar Island.

I shrug and open my hands. "Life moves on, like a river flowing, as your father used to say. Meet my new friends, Mercury Thunder and Del Witherspoon."

She shakes their hands and glances at the door. "I brought food. Does anyone want to help me bring it in?"

I clap a hand to my chest. "Oh good, because I only made turkey sandwiches."

My daughter beams. "We brought a feast, so we should be set, except for drinks."

A smile spreads across my face, pleased that she's here with my grandson. "I've got that covered."

We're about to go out to Rose's car when there's a knock on the door using Mary's code of three short knocks, a pause and a loud one. I say, "Excuse me," hurrying to the door and opening it wide. Mary and Fred are wearing red scarves, red hats, and blue puffer jackets. I grin at my friends. "Come in, you two. I was just introducing everyone. Rose and Max are here too.""

Mary and Fred step inside, and their eyes grow wide when they see Mercury and Del standing in the living room. I take their coats, and Mary says, "Did you both leave Shore Lodge today with Jacklyn on Irena's boat?"

Mercury chuckles and flashes me a smile. I haven't introduced him to my friends yet and had planned to over dinner this evening. I say, "Mercury and I met when Jack

Fishbone was in trouble and a debt collector threatened his life." Mercury shakes their hands.

I turn to the man from Shore Lodge, who steps forward to shake Mary and Fred's hands. He says, "I'm Del Witherspoon, and I saw Jacklyn leaving Shore Lodge with her friends, so I ran down to the dock to catch a ride to town with them. We met when I was at Shore Lodge."

My daughter turns to Mercury and Del. "Hi, I'm Rose, Jacklyn's daughter, and this is Max."

Max grins and scampers off to the kitchen with my dog following close behind. They're such an adorable pair. Max knows I keep the dog treats in a cupboard. I hear a stool scrape across the floor as Max moves it to reach the box. "Only one," I call to him, loving the chaos and commotion my grandson brings when he visits.

"I know, grandma."

Rose says, "I brought food for dinner. Anyone want to help me bring it in?"

Max pops out of the kitchen. "I do."

We all troop outside in gusting wind and driving sleet and snow. Night is falling, even though it's late afternoon. We carry cardboard boxes with containers of potato salad, macaroni salad, salad greens, two long loaves of bread, and fried chicken. I set the bucket of chicken down on the kitchen counter and inhale the tantalizing smell.

I say, "Rose, it was so thoughtful of you to bring all this. Thank you!"

She grins. "I wasn't sure if you'd be making dinner, so I thought I'd bring it with us."

"I picked out the chicken," Max says, sniffing the air.

"Well, you did a good job," I say. "Why don't we all settle in, and I'll see what else I can rustle up for a meal."

Mary says, "I'll serve drinks."

Rose nods. "I'll set the table. Do you have more chairs, Mom?"

"Sure, in the garage I have folding chairs from when I got home after your brother emptied out my house."

Rose purses her lips. "I still can't believe he did that to you. I'm so sorry that I went along with his plan. It was selfish of me not to pay attention. I feel so awful about what happened to you."

I pat her shoulder. "Don't worry about it. The whole experience made me stronger. I won't fall for his B.S. again."

The floor shakes under my feet, windows rattle and a loud boom comes from out front of the house. My body tenses, and I whip my head around. "What was that? It sounded like an explosion."

I fling open the front door and run outside. My jaw drops at the sight of a billowing cloud of white-gray smoke. I bet my son had something to do with this.

56

DEL

Sleet hits the windows in Jacklyn's house, and I rub my arms, wishing for a moment that I was in Shore Lodge, where I admitted myself to the first-floor resident program for depression and grief. I felt better after living there a few months and thought I'd be fine returning to the real world. But now I'm lost at sea, surrounded by warm, kind people who are doing me an enormous favor by giving me a place to sleep and promising to help me find my way.

My stomach knots at the prospect of starting over. Now that I'm on this side of Cedar Channel, I'm starting to doubt I have the strength to begin again after retirement and my dear wife's death.

My eyes glaze over when introductions are made to Jacklyn's daughter and grandson and her friends. Everyone seems comfortable in this group except for me.

I'm out of my element, having been encased in a quiet cocoon of sadness for the last year. I haven't even picked up my trumpet to practice, like I did every day. It's been that bad.

A loud noise snaps me out of my reverie. Walls of the house shake, window panes rattle and a framed photo on the wall tilts. My body tenses, ready for a fight, and I follow Jacklyn, racing outside. A mud-splattered white truck drives away, and Jacklyn shakes a fist, yelling, "Dusty!"

I put my hands on my knees, breathing hard, and shake my head. I'd better not get involved with this woman, even though she's about my age and she was kind to me from the get-go when I came running down to the dock in a panic to get off Cedar Island. Jacklyn's family is screwy and something smells off, with her son being so angry with her and her not knowing her daughter was coming for dinner.

I straighten up and take a deep breath of briny sea air wafting off the channel. I'll ride out my welcome for a while, get my feet under me and observe their crazy family dynamics. I don't need to get involved after what I've been through. I left that behind when I crossed over on the ferry to Cedar Island the first time.

57

———

MERCURY

An explosion outside reverberates, making the floor shake beneath my feet. Glasses set out on the counter vibrate, and I swallow hard, reminded of my time in a battle-torn war, a period I vowed to put in the past and forget. I release a shaky breath, and my armpits prickle with sweat. My hands are clenched, fingernails digging into my palms. I tell myself to snap out of it and look around Jacklyn's house. She runs outside and I bolt, following her.

An enormous hazy cloud of smoke floats over the lawn and is spreading, coming our way. A dented white truck drives off, and Jacklyn yells and shakes a fist at the driver.

I say, "That was a powerful firework."

She stares down the street as the truck rounds the

corner and shakes her head. "I'm calling the police. That was my son who set it off."

Rose stands near the door, shielding her son from unknown harm with her arms around him. Max squirms and pulls away, running to inspect the cloud of smoke.

Jacklyn says, "Everyone inside, please. I'll call the cops on my son."

Rose cocks her head. "You think Dusty did this?"

Jacklyn nods and points down the street. "He definitely did. He just drove off in his truck."

Mary says, "You've been through so much, are you sure it was him?"

Jacklyn's cheeks flush, and she pulls out her phone. "I'm sure, so don't doubt me. I know my own son. He was grinning as he drove away, and this means war."

Rose says, "The noise scared me."

Max looks up at his mom. "Is Uncle Dusty dangerous?"

Rose says, "We'll talk about it later."

"I want to talk about it now," Max says.

Rose shushes him, leaning over and patting his chest, and I focus my attention on the cloud of smoke. I say to Rose, "Go inside and keep the windows and doors closed."

While Jacklyn is on the phone, Mary, Fred, Del and I walk around the edges of the cloud, scouring the yard in growing darkness for the source of the smoke. My heart is racing, hairs on my arms stand on end, and sweat drips down my arms, despite the chill in the air.

I stop and cough, saying, "The smoke's too thick to see what made it."

Staring down the street where the truck took off, I shake my head. Who would do this to a family member, especially to such a kind person like Jacklyn? I bite my lip. I'm not sure what this is all about. Is it Jacklyn's fault that her son is angry with her? Mothers can be blamed for their children's problems, but I have a hunch his attitude and actions aren't related to how she raised him.

***

JACKLYN

I call the police and hang up, standing in the dark with my hands on my hips, surveying the yard and breathing smoke-filled air. Snowflakes fall, dusting the yard, and a blast of frigid air blows past. A street light illuminates a section of street where Dusty left fresh black tire marks when he raced off. I let out a long sigh of sadness. My son has become a wounded, dangerous man.

A hush falls over the area, and we're in a peaceful snow scene but with a smoke bomb on the front lawn. Front doors open and neighbors pour out of their homes. A police car rounds the corner, coming down the block. A next-door neighbor steps outside, letting the storm door slap behind her. She hurries over. "What happened?"

I rub my hands together for warmth as snowflakes drift past. "My son set off a smoke bomb."

She tilts her head. "He must really be mad about something."

"He wanted to come over for dinner."

Her eyebrows arch. "He did that over a missed dinner invite? Is that all it took? Families, who needs them."

I nod. "Families can be strange."

58

DUSTY

My windshield wipers whine, and I make my way west on Highway 20, retracing my steps. The windshield is fogged, making it difficult to view the road ahead, and I rub it with my sleeve to see better.

The smoke bomb made the most satisfying boom, bigger and better than with fireworks I've used before. The guy I met playing pool heard my story about wanting to get revenge, and he offered me a smoke bomb he bought for Fourth of July but never used, stored in the trunk of his car.

I laughed when the smoke bomb blew up on Mom's lawn, but now the adrenaline rush is gone, and a hollow feeling remains. I'm alone and abandoned by my mom, my father who died, my sister, and the guys at the tavern who I thought were my friends.

I shake my head, reminded of grade school when I was blamed for breaking into a house under construction. My buddy dared me to go with him, so I followed. But when we were caught, my mom believed my friend when he said it was my idea and sided against me. I've been the black sheep of the family for as long as I can remember.

My stomach growls. The only food at the musty cabin is a box of half-empty stale crackers and some moldy cheddar cheese. I should turn around and head back to Mom's. I'll barge in like I belong there and interrupt her party.

Approaching the foothills, the air is colder and snow accumulates on the sides of the road. I clench my teeth, swerving to avoid a piece of a blown tire, and a memory flits past. On Christmas Eve when we were kids, my sister stabbed me with a fondue fork. It dug in and dangled from my cheek, and I ran screaming to my mother, who was in the kitchen. "Look what Rose did to me!" Instead of scolding Rose, she said, "You must've deserved it."

Bottled rage bubbles up, building inside. My grip on the steering wheel tightens. I shouldn't be hungry and alone on a holiday. I stomp on the gas pedal and scream, blaming everyone for my sorry predicament.

My truck shudders and swerves, fishtailing on black ice. My pulse races, and I yelp, tapping on the brakes and turning the steering wheel, hands slick with sweat. The truck spins around and comes to a stop pointing in the direction of Millersville.

My heart pounds in my chest. I wipe sweat from my brow and blow out a breath. "This must be a sign. Her guests will have another helping of Dusty over dinner tonight."

I start down the road to my mother's home, hunched over the wheel, filled with ill will. Fondue forks can be used for more than skewering a brother or a piece of bread. It's time I took my revenge to the next level.

59

JACKLYN

I stand outside with my arms crossed, waiting for the police officer and tapping a toe, fuming at my son. It was a long enough day without his shenanigans. My husband made a huge mistake by coddling Dusty and feeding the hungry beast, giving him money.

I cock my head, because I'm also to blame for not keeping a careful watch over our bank balances. I let Albert handle the finances, but now I know better and it's too late to change the course of our winding river.

The air is crisp and cold. The wind whips up snow from the ground, blowing it in my eyes and making trees moan and sway. An officer in blue climbs out of a police car and lumbers toward my house. Neighbors crowd around, pointing at the cloud of smoke.

I stride over the officer and introduce myself. "I'm

Jacklyn Stone, and I called about a smoke bomb set off in my yard."

He adjusts his cap and says, "I'll take a look around."

Christmas carols drift from a nearby house, creating a harsh contrast to what happened here, which is madness unleashed and revenge born out of conceit. I let out a sigh and wish, for the hundredth time, that my husband was alive and by my side. He wasn't perfect, and neither am I, but he encouraged our son's frequent requests to keep his business afloat. Don't water a garden you don't want to grow, for goodness sake.

A strange woman steps out of a house next door like she owns the place. Where are my neighbors who owned it? I go over to the woman, who is wrapped in a thick black shawl embroidered with peacocks with colorful plumes, and say, "I'm Jacklyn Stone, and I live next door. Are you new here?"

She says, "I'm Zoila, Kirk's ex-wife."

"What happened to my neighbors who lived here?"

She shrugs. "Kirk offered them enough money so they left and rented it to me fully furnished. I've been sick, and he wants to take care of me."

I cock my head. "Isn't Kirk married?"

She says, "Sure, but that doesn't mean we can't be friends and live next door."

I open my hands. "Whatever works. Welcome to the neighborhood."

My dog runs up to me and rubs against my leg, and I

pet him while the officer marches around my yard inspecting. Buddy looks at me with big questioning brown eyes, and I pat his chest, telling him to go with Max, who is hopping on one leg, watching the police officer.

Mercury, Del, Rose, Mary and Fred gather around me. Staring at the dark sky, I shrug at how worked up I was about conducting an environmental survey before my building permit could be approved. I look around and realize my business worries pale before the importance of appreciating friends. I'll celebrate with them tonight and be grateful we went back to Shore Lodge and made it home alive. I'll forget the dastardly deed my son did on my front lawn.

I march over to the officer and ask, "What do you think did it, Officer?"

He hitches up his pants. "I think it was a very powerful smoke bomb."

"I saw my son driving away from the scene of the crime."

His eyebrows shoot up. "Can you prove he did it?"

I shake my head. "No, I can't."

"Our hands are tied then. I've got enough for my report, and I'll go back to the station and write it up. Good night, and Merry Christmas."

As he walks to his car, I give my daughter a hug. "Thank you for coming to see me tonight. I was depressed after your dad died, and I appreciate you hanging out with your old mom."

She laughs. "There's nothing old about you. You still have your fire and spunk."

A grin spreads across my face. "I'm glad to hear that, and if Dusty tries to convince you I'm out of my mind and need to be locked up, tell him the truth. I'm right as rain now."

We walk toward the house, arm in arm. Snow flies in my eyes, and I squint to see better. She says, "We dealt with dad's death differently and that pulled us apart. I was distracted, you were down in the dumps, and Dusty got angry. Do you think he'll calm down and get back to his laid-back self?"

I grimace and shake my head. "Darling dearest one, I don't believe that'll ever happen. When your dad went to the grave, it seems he took your brother's good nature with him."

She pats my shoulder. "This must be hard on you. I hope he'll come around."

I pause at the threshold and say, ""I left my hopes for your brother changing for the better years ago, when you father took me on a surprise vacation to Paris, Idaho."

Rose gives me a tight smile. "What happened?"

I roll my eyes. "Dusty called to demand we come home. He was broke and needed money for a fishing trip with his buddies from the tavern. But he was twenty-five years old, didn't live at home, and he called at one in the morning at the hotel. That's when I knew we had trouble on our hands." I wipe a tear from my eye and gesture inside. "Come on, let's get warm and have dinner with these wonderful people."

Inside, I add, "I'm not going to worry about Dusty and his problems. I need to separate myself emotionally to survive."

Fred wanders over with a celery stick in his hand. "Pretty grim talk for a holiday, isn't it?"

I open my hands and glance at my new friend Mercury, who radiates concern. "It is grim talk, but I have a whole new future to look forward to." I open my arms wide and say, "Right now, my future is in Stone Estates."

We find beverages and raise our glasses. "To Stone Estates."

Mary says, "And to deliriously happy times for Jacklyn, who deserves joy every minute."

I nod and smile, letting out a contented sigh. This is where I belong. My grandson appears by my side, sliding an arm around my waist. "I love you grandma."

Tears trickle down my cheeks. "I love you too, sweat peach."

Everyone talks at once, going in the kitchen and bringing out food, but Max and I stand there in our bubble of love, his hot hand warming my side. He says, "I'll go help and you can stay here. Mom says you deserve to rest after what Uncle Dusty did to you."

I bend over and kiss the top of his head that smells like a fresh-baked loaf of bread just pulled from the oven. "I'll help too."

I step into the kitchen, and the comforting buzz of conversations surround me. This is my new life, rooted firmly with the space to spread my branches in the months ahead.

I give my dog a celebratory scoop of kibble and jump into the fray, carrying a platter of crackers and a bowl of artichoke dip to the table. As I set down items on the table, a shiver runs through me, and I glance outside. Nothing will destroy my peace tonight. All is quiet and calm.

Soon, our group is gathered around the dining table sipping wine and beer, or in my case, a French 75 cocktail. I raise my glass in a toast and say, "Here's to friends and family and to those we love who couldn't be with us tonight."

Rose gives me a strange look and sips her white wine. "Here's to forgiveness and thankfulness."

I send her an air kiss and sip my drink. "And most important of all, here's to the best group of people I could spend tonight with. Thank you for being here and sharing my home."

Mercury and I exchange a quick look and a feeling of warmth floods through me. He smiles and says, as others join in, "Here, here! Thanks for hosting us."

A sound from the house next door makes me jump up and peer out my window. The new woman who moved in, displacing my long-time neighbors, is playing loud music with her front door open while she sweeps her front porch in see-through white lingerie. I slide into my seat at the table and say, "I think my new neighbor is a bit strange."

Rose waves my concerns away. "Forget about it. You have enough on your mind with your new subdivision. Everyone has an odd neighbor."

I nod but deep inside, I have a feeling I should keep an eye on my new neighbor. Something isn't right.

Max says, "Yeah, grandma, go build some houses, and I'll help you, so I can live in one of them some day. I want to grow up and build houses, just like you and Uncle Dusty."

Rose and I glance at each other, and I purse my lips, not uttering a word against Dusty in front of the child. I swallow fears that my son might return with vengeance on his mind and spoil our evening. Smiling at the others gathered around my new long table, I settle back in my chair with a contented sigh, surrounded by love.

60

IRENA

I drive away from the café and smile, eager to see my daughter. Snowflakes drift down, leaving a light dusting of white on lawns. I push on the gas pedal, and a stab of guilt twists in my gut. A good mother would've stayed home with her teenage daughter baking Christmas cookies. But Jacklyn needed me to take her to Cedar Island, and I wanted to help. We did bring a Shore Lodge resident back to town, so we sort of accomplished what we set out to do.

I shrug and park in my driveway, glancing at my dark house with a frown. Kelly should be home with the lights on. I hop out of the car and run to the front door, which is ajar. I run through the house calling for Kelly, but she doesn't answer. She's not in the living room, kitchen, bathroom or her bedroom.

I say in a loud voice, "Kels, where are you? I'm home."

On the kitchen table is a note scrawled with a black marker. I recognize the writing from my childhood and my heart sinks as I read: 'You didn't let me see Kelly, so I took her with me. Don't call the police. Dad.'

My hands tremble, and I drop the note on the table, bursting into tears. If I'd been home with Kelly, he wouldn't have had a chance to take her. This is my fault.

Weeping, I clench my hands and scream before telling myself to snap out of it. I've got to do something to find her. Wiping snot from my nose, I grab my phone and call Violet.

She picks up right away, and country music blares in the background.

"Merry Christmas. What's up?"

"My father took Kelly. I've got to find her."

She says to someone on the other end, "Turn the music down. Kelly's been taken."

Thank you for reading *The Winter Storm*! Please let other readers know what to expect by posting ratings and reviews on Goodreads, Amazon and BookBub.

Next up is *The Cold Night!*

Jacklyn's story starts in *Shore Lodge!*
A grieving widow is tricked into going to a retreat center,
which turns out to be a secure psychiatric unit.
She must escape to rescue her dog and reclaim her home.
My Book

Books about Jacklyn's friends:

For Irena's story, read *Under Jackson Bridge, Missing Man and By Midnight.*

For Karina's story, read *Secrets at the Café.*

For Violet's story, read *The Mother's Threat.*

Don't miss news about my book releases and deals! Sign up at my website www.susanspechtoram.com for my author newsletter.

Follow me on BookBub for updates: https://www.bookbub.com/authors/susan-specht-oram

My Facebook author page is Susan Specht Oram Author

Check out my YouTube channel to see the setting for my novels: (@susanspechtoramauthor).

Thank you for reading my books!

ABOUT THE AUTHOR

Susan writes mysteries-thrillers with high stakes and heart set in a fictional Pacific Northwest small town. Previously, she served as senior director of corporate communications for biotechnology companies. Susan worked as an activity aide in an upscale nursing home's secure psychiatric unit. She was a potter and painter with an art studio in Seattle and also worked as a market researcher, a nurse's aide, a waitress, and a library page. Her essays have been published in Mothering Magazine, Twins Magazine and Utne Reader.

Susan grew up near Detroit, Michigan and received a BFA with Honors from University of Oregon and a MBA from Seattle University. She lives in a windy part of the Pacific Northwest with her husband and their rescue dog.

f

BOOKS BY SUSAN SPECHT ORAM

Shore Lodge

The Thieves

Cabin Eight

Secrets at the Café

The Mother's Threat

Under Jackson Bridge

Missing Man

By Midnight

The Winter Storm

The Cold Night

Humorous fiction:

Boating with Buddy, a report from a canine correspondent

Nonfiction:

Brief business books on investor relations, crisis
communication and public relations